Ivor Tymchak has been at va
writer of a strip cartoon that a
man for a rock band, a grapl
speaker, a presentation skills t
founder and organizer of Bettakuncha.

His favourite piece of trivia to drop at parties (which he rarely attends because no one invites him) is that he was at the Sex Pistols' last UK gig, in Huddersfield on Christmas Day, 1977.

Ivor's previous publications include the comic book *Life and How to Live It*, the film *How to Care for Your Hamsters*, and a children's book, *Maggie, the Magpie that Couldn't Fly*.

Sex & Death

& Other Stories

Ivor Tymchak

Published by Armley Press, 2019
ISBN 978-1-9160165-1-4

Acknowledgements

Copy editing: John Lake
Cover design: Ivor Tymchak
Cover compositing: Mick Lake
Layout: Ian Dobson
Production: Mick McCann

Thanks to Susan Williamson, without whom this book probably wouldn't exist. She encouraged my writing from the start and fiercely critiqued each story. I also need to thank Wakefield Word, my writers' group, for its support.

I dedicate this book to all artists and writers who come from a working-class background

Twitter: @ivortymchak

Contents

Sex and Death

The impression I get when I talk to my neighbours is that the war is starting to lose its appeal. The state media isn't reporting the easy victories with the same frequency as it used to do and deprivations are beginning to bite deeper every day. We are now being urged to help the war effort by growing our own vegetables using any bit of garden we might have. This suggests the fighting is going to go on for a lot longer than the politicians have led us to believe – do they learn nothing from history?

I had already converted my back garden into a vegetable patch before the war started. I didn't have any special insight into its outbreak (I'm not that astute), it's just that I was already fighting a different war – one against the pesticides and chemicals that farmers habitually put on their crops. It's one thing when an enemy tries to kill you with bullets and bombs but quite another when your own farmers try to poison you.

It's July and the height of the growing season. I am being kept busy each evening weeding or watering the plants. Pest control is on high alert too. Most nights I'm in the garden around midnight armed with a flashlight and spade, hunting for the army of slugs that emerge from their hiding places at dusk. If rain fell earlier in the day they are easier to find as the light shines off their glistening bodies. A swift drop of the spade blade is all it takes to execute them. Despite my best efforts though they still take their toll on my crops; I can't kill them fast enough

I've just done the routine day patrol of all my plants and now I'm resting in the old wooden garden chair positioned in the shade of the plum tree. With smug satisfaction I'm surveying all that I have cultivated this

7

year: beans, parsnips, broccoli, potatoes. The lush, variegated bed of green foliage is given centre stage and set off by an unblemished backdrop of clear blue sky graduating from intense cobalt blue at the top to a metallic cyan at the bottom. Birds sing, bees hum and such is the tranquillity of the moment that I decide to break open the last bottle of homemade wine I still have from before the war. I was saving it for a special occasion, and this magical moment, so perfect in its ordinariness, is as good a time as any.

I go into the house to retrieve the bottle from the back of the pantry. A single dusty cobweb line trails from its neck like an abandoned rope left by a miniature abseiler long since gone after their mysterious mission. From a kitchen cupboard I get out a glass and from a drawer, a corkscrew. The cork slides perfectly out of the neck of the bottle and emerges like a fat new-born grub with a satisfying *plop*. I take the bottle and the glass into the garden and retake my seat under the tree that donated the original fruit for the wine. On a little trestle table next to the chair I place the bottle and I begin to enjoy the distilled nectar. The first sip invigorates my body and reminds me that I need to do another task later on – spread a bag of blood and bone meal fertilizer onto the vegetable patch.

I'm on my second glass of wine and beginning to feel deliciously drowsy when in the periphery of my vision there is a small flash of white. Something primitive fires off in the reptilian part of my brain and I'm suddenly alert.

In the shimmering air a cabbage-white butterfly dances provocatively above my purple-sprouting broccoli plants.

I'm watching this display of intent with growing alarm. I know from experience that the butterfly will

8

soon alight on one of the defenceless turquoise leaves of the broccoli and, on the underside of it, lay a cluster of eggs like so many tiny grenades. Because I don't use any pesticides all such eggs have to be scraped off by hand or harvested by natural predators so I have my usual reflex urge to jump up, rush at the butterfly like a charging infantryman and wave it away from the garden before it can complete its mission; but the wine I've just enjoyed has ambushed that reflex midway between my brain and my legs and, like a wily old ambassador, detained it with soothing incantations about how wonderful it is to be alive; and some things just aren't worth the candle...

So, with a resigned air, I give the butterfly a temporary pass.

And then, out of the sky, another butterfly appears and at a stroke doubles my anxiety. But almost immediately, a third butterfly joins the dance and my alarm switches gratefully to curiosity – such a grouping means more than just the routine laying of eggs. I sense the new arrival is going to cut in on the dance.

Sure enough, I intuitively recognize the primitive, timeless moves of a courtship display between the butterflies. Every human male is familiar with the posturing displays of other males vying for the sexual favours of a female, whatever the species.

The female butterfly settles on the patch of green lawn immediately adjacent to the broccoli plants and disports herself invitingly for the males. One of them attempts to land on her back to mate but the other male interferes and the two take to the air to do battle.

My curiosity aroused now, I stand up unsteadily and walk the few paces into the lawn to get a closer look. The female is only slightly perturbed by my appearance and flies a couple of feet further along the lawn before settling on the grass again. I shadow her move and step closer to her but this time she is content to lie on the grass, such is her urgent imperative for sex.

One of the males has by now won the effeminate duel of wing slapping and descends on her open and welcoming back. As they mate I watch their intimacy.

The countless offspring of these insects will eat my food, that fact is undeniable. As beautiful as they are in their design and movement I can't rid myself of the selfish idea that I should protect what is mine and kill them.

I continue to watch their mating, my feet only inches from their copulating bodies. My intoxicated brain makes a clumsy poetic exploration into the two most powerful forces in nature; sex and death and attempts to reconcile them. If I stepped on the butterflies now they would experience both states simultaneously. How perfect would that be?

A sober me would no doubt have let them perform their mating and then I would have shooed them away afterwards in a delusional belief that they would show their gratitude by not returning to my territory and pillaging the bounty I'd produced. But the wine has done its damage and in the long, sad history of that terrible drug it momentarily facilitates my base instincts. Taking me by surprise – my moral considerations suddenly swept aside like a wooden beach hut in a tsunami – I witness my foot, armoured in scarred old leather, shoot forward and land firmly on the copulating pair.

With a pang of guilt I instantly withdraw my foot but the two white butterflies lie inert among the leaves of grass, dead as petals. The opportunistic second male butterfly sees its chance and returns, dancing to within a few inches of the female, but then must catch a sharp scent of death because it quickly departs for good.

I return to my seat to consider my actions. I'm troubled by my wildly fluctuating moral compass – why am I able to despatch slugs so easily but not butterflies?

Several minutes later, I'm distracted from my reverie by a tell-tale buzzing sound. I look up to see that the drama has not yet ended. Two wasps hover like malevolent angels over the carcasses of the butterflies. They set down on their victims and immediately begin to butcher them.

Again, curiosity gets the better of me and I step forward to witness this new act. With ruthless efficiency the wasps neatly saw off the wings, then carry the bodies aloft and away like freshly harvested souls for the waiting hell that is the wasps' nest.

Nothing is wasted in nature. The circle is renewed: the bodies of the butterflies will give birth to new life but not in the form of caterpillars. A predator species will flourish instead, designed to hunt and kill the defenceless offspring of the *cabbage white*.

Then, still standing at the scene of the slaughter on my lawn, I hear another faint but powerful droning sound. It is as if a swarm of monstrous bees is slowly filling the air. A primitive fear grips my intestines. I know I should run but the wine has dulled my senses and I jerk my head up in wild panic to scan the heavens. And there in the distance I see them. I keep my eyes fixed on the rough, dark line in the sky getting nearer and wider. The droning sound grows in intensity until it is an all-consuming roar – my empty wine glass trembles faintly on the trestle table.

The sky darkens and I look directly overhead at the heavy layer of bombers creeping across the sky like a swiftly moving stain of blood. I relax – they're *our* bombers, on their way to a distant shore to inflict unimaginable carnage. Collectively, they look like the underside of a giant boot poised to crush an unsuspecting town where the inhabitants might be dancing, courting, making love...

I think of the man controlling the boot, drunk with insane power.

Why Stan Barstow Never Moved from Wakefield

The canopy of lime trees on Goring Park Avenue produces a kaleidoscope of shifting spots of sunlight in the road as I walk. The quiet street looks pleasant enough now but I'm familiar with its sordid past. I'm looking for Goring House and I find it only sixty yards from the junction with Teall Street. It looks imposing with its broad, stone mullioned bay windows. Its grandeur is doubly emphasized by the juxtaposition of more modest houses neighbouring it.

I'm here to see Stan Barstow, who now lives in the house, although he doesn't know I intend to call on him. He hasn't responded to the letter and manuscript I sent him several weeks ago. I'm beginning to learn that this is not an unusual occurrence – writers rarely, if ever, respond to unsolicited manuscripts but I assumed that the Wakefield postcode I'd hand written on my return envelope would at least have piqued his interest.

I approach the corner of the small front garden facing the street. There is no sign of life from anywhere around the house or in any of the windows. He could be out, of course, possibly even out of the country now he's achieved such success, but I felt I had to take some kind of positive action if only to delude myself my life was going somewhere. The more I think about it, the more stupid is my idea to call unannounced. How is he going to react when a poor wannabe writer pitches up on his doorstep? Would he be flattered? Annoyed? Glad of the respite it offered him from the daily grind of bashing out two thousand words a day (or however many he sets himself) on his typewriter?

I hesitate near the large stone gateposts. I can't help admiring the house; it does what it was intended to do – suggest a bright future full of grand parties and lively conversations.

It was built and paid for by John Tennant, who had been suckered into a doomed scheme dreamt up by Mathew Wharton in the 1880s. Less than a mile away from the house is Ossett spa, a water source that some people thought could germinate the seeds of growth in the area to match that of another spa town – Harrogate. And Harrogate was the vision that Wharton sold to anyone who would listen to him; he managed to convince Tennant that if the infrastructure were built around the water source the tourists would surely come.

Alas, the allure of Ossett proved resistible for the general public and the fortunes of Tennant began to wane. Eventually when all hope of a building boom had faded and the finances of Tennant were examined they proved wanting. He was ruined. Rather than face the humiliation of debt, he took his own life aged 49 inside the house that Stan Barstow now composes his stories in. Harrogate, of course, became grander and wealthier but poor Ossett had to make do with mungo and shoddy along with utilitarian engineering for the railways. At least the railway industry in Ossett managed to manufacture Barstow.

I glance at the upstairs windows and try to imagine in which one of the bedrooms Tennant had hung himself. How do prospective buyers view a house that has had an untimely death in it? Murder must be the worst; ghosts can't be too far away when such a crime has been committed. I guess writers appreciate that kind of history.

I have spent far too long watching the house and I'm beginning to feel conspicuous. For any neighbours that might be twitching their net curtains and peering into the street I imagine that I must be looking like some apprentice burglar loitering outside a property and sizing it up for a future break-in. A slimy dampness lubricates my armpits and I'm becoming increasingly nervous. As a twenty year old I'm still as gauche as when I was an adolescent schoolboy.

What if he thinks my writing is shit? Would he say as much or would he be too embarrassed to say so?

That's if he's even read the bloody thing.

Bollocks! It's do or die. I stride up to the black wooden door and lift the doorknocker. I hesitate momentarily before I let it fall against the anvil.

After a few seconds I'm telling myself no one is home and I can go now, back to my terraced house in Gawthorpe, but I know I should try once more at least. *Once more with conviction,* I tell myself.

BOOM! goes the doorknocker and I jump back in astonishment at the noise I've just made. I'm terrified it will be misinterpreted by the occupant as a summons by impatient bailiffs or police.

Several seconds pass. Nothing. No one home.

Simultaneously relieved and disappointed I quickly exit the gate and head off down the street. At the junction I turn left and start walking into Ossett.

It's a couple of miles' walk into Ossett and as I head up the gently sloping hill of Station Road I remember that one of the first shops I will encounter before entering the town centre properly is Funny Foods, a health food shop. I remember that I need some dates and whole-wheat flour for my bread making. I check my finances and calculate that I have enough money. I also calculate that the weight of the goods won't be too heavy to hamper my walk home to Gawthorpe – another two miles on the other side of Ossett.

As I enter the shop a bell suspended over the entrance gives a hugely satisfying ring – it's just like the sound effect the BBC use in a radio play or comedy sketch show (Woman enters shop: *sound F/X of bell ringing*).

The shop is quiet, as it usually is during the week. 'Healthy foods' is still a bit of a novelty in these parts and only hippies and educated middle-class types buy them. I know where the dates are kept and I look for the friendly middle-aged woman who runs the shop, as she is required to dig them out of a large plastic bag housed in a wooden bin. Near the counter I see her chatting to a tall man who has his back to me. There is something odd about her behaviour. I've never seen her so obsequious with a customer before, like she's in the presence of royalty or a man she finds sexually attractive. Money changes hands over the counter and the woman chants an oft-repeated *au revoir* to the man, who turns towards me to head for the exit. The man is elegantly dressed in a beige jacket and his long face is wearing a thin, dark moustache. I immediately recognize him – Stan Barstow. Being the only other customer in the shop he looks directly at me as he passes. He divines I've recognized him and half expects some kind of acknowledgement from me. I'm too dumbstruck with the coincidence to make any outward sign. He's out of the door before I come to my senses and I quickly follow him out – the doorbell clattering maniacally as if expressing its annoyance at being made to work so hard in so short a space of time.

'Mr Barstow!' I shout. He stops and turns towards me showing no emotion. His hand begins seeking something in his jacket pocket.

'Yes?'

'I've just come from your house' – an expression of alarm flits over his face – 'but you weren't in.'

'Indeed' he says, 'that's because I was here. How can I help you?'

'I… I was just calling to see if you'd read my manuscript that I posted to you last month. I just wanted some feedback on it.'

A weary look then invades his face, which he does his best to hide, and his hand stops the automatic search for a pen. 'What's your name?'

'Ivor – Ivor Tymchak,' I answer hopefully.

'All right, Ivor, I have to tell you now that I receive many unsolicited scripts and I'm a busy man being a full-time writer so as you can imagine, reading any of them would take up a lot of valuable time. As a result I've had to make a blanket decision – as many writers do – to never read unsolicited scripts, it's simply too troublesome.'

He delivers these lines effortlessly as if he's spoken them many times before and I silently stare at him waiting for the rest of the polite brush-off he surely issues with every such encounter. He hesitates, and then takes a quick look at his wristwatch.

'But look, I tell you what, I've got half an hour to spare before I need to be somewhere else and you've gone to the trouble to find me in person so I'll let you have that time to talk to me about writing if that's what you want. How does that sound?'

'Er, that's great. Thanks!'

'Let's grab a coffee in the tea rooms near the arcade.' And with that we stride off together in the direction of Prospect Street.

In the café we talk for a while about general writing matters until Stan divines my inattentiveness and cuts to the chase.

'Why have you sought me out, Ivor? I sense there's more on your mind than just the craft of writing.'

Shocked, I ask myself how he could sense that I have a secret fear driving my actions, then I realize that's why some people are gifted writers – they can easily see through the facades people try to contrive for themselves. And so, disarmed so easily, I confess my real reason for wanting to speak to him.

'You've made it, Stan, you're famous and respected as a writer. Why are you still in Wakefield?'

'Don't you like Wakefield?'

'Not really. It's nowhere, nothing exciting goes on here – culturally I mean. That's why everyone moves to London when they get the chance. I don't want to be a nobody.'

He gives me a severe look and I suddenly realise I might have insulted him by implying he's a nobody too. He takes a sip of his tepid coffee before he speaks.

'A nobody, eh? All my life I've battled against this attitude. Coming from a working-class background as I do, I discovered you're almost taught to think of yourself as a nobody. And even as my novel *A Kind of Loving* achieved the success it did, I couldn't get the recognition of that achievement from my peers. You're considered a kind of freak when you achieve something that they think you're not entitled to.

'I did think about moving to London several times but I realised my material is mined from these working-class seams. If I leave all that behind it's reinforcing the idea that the provinces are culturally barren and hold no interest for a curious mind. By moving away I'd be adding to the myth that the working classes are not worth bothering with and that simply isn't true. There's many a working-class boy or girl who is just as capable as any middle-class child but they're not given the opportunity to flourish.'

His expression took on a pained look as if he were remembering some boyhood friends who must have displayed promising talent before they were forced into the railway industry or down the coalmines.

He continued: 'You want to "escape" Wakefield but the truth is you want to escape your roots. I sense you're ashamed of them. Even if you were to move to London you can't hide from your gut convictions or sense of identity. True, you would meet some interesting people there, some crazy people... but most of us live humdrum lives punctuated by births, deaths and marriages.

'Trust me, Ivor; there is nothing wrong with Wakefield or even Horbury, where I spent most of my childhood. Life stories aren't portioned out like gifts on a Christmas morning to eager children with the quality of those stories being completely dependent on the wealth or class of the household. No, stories come from human beings and they're everywhere in all shapes and sizes dressed in the most unassuming of garments – there's even a couple sitting right here at this table. What stories might *they* tell one day?'

*

It's decades later and I'm in Horbury sitting on one of the wooden benches situated in a little green space that bulges out from Queen Street, reminiscing about that encounter with Stan. The summer sun is warming the back of my head as I watch the actors of real life striding on the concrete and tarmac stage in front of me going about their daily business.

I still live in Wakefield but my regret of not moving away to somewhere more exciting is slowly diminishing. Since that conversation with Stan my writing got nowhere apart from the odd short story. It's taken me a long time to realize the wisdom in his words – you can travel the world over but the essence of what makes life interesting resides inside of you. Sharing that essence with others is what makes life worth living.

I get up, roused from my reverie by the bells of St Peter and St Leonard's church – situated just a few metres up the hill – striking 3 p.m. The church was a gift to the village of Horbury from John Carr, the local-born architect who went on to design Harewood House. But that's another story for another day.

I leave my seat in the carefully tended space now known as Stan Barstow Garden and walk up the hill towards my local library.

The Gospel According to Alex

'Alex, can I interrupt you, please?'

This came from Tony, a short, white-haired man with the kind of brown, weather-beaten, face that signifies decades of outdoor activity. He was smiling when he said this but Tony smiled after everything he said so it was impossible to tell what the emotion was behind the request. Standing next to him was Jack, the young, earnest vicar, who wasn't smiling at all as he looked at me.

I put down the three, stacked chairs I was carrying. I was in the middle of helping two other middle-aged helpers clear the church hall after the meeting of lonely old Christian women (although it was more politely called 'Women of Faith' in the activity list). The next activity in the hall was the yoga class at 2pm.

'Of course,' I said. 'Is anything wrong?'

'No, no,' said Tony. 'We'd just like to talk with you if that's okay.'

I looked at Jack, who now initiated a brief stretching of his lips. Tony raised his hand and with his palm upwards pointed to a door in the wall of the hall. 'Shall we go into the office? It's quieter,' he said.

There was some scraping of chair legs and chatter from the other helpers in the hall but nothing so loud that it could drown out any kind of normal conversation so the invitation to enter the office suggested that something serious or at least sensitive was going to be discussed.

'Of course,' I said, 'I'll just stack these chairs away first and I'll see you in there.'

Once we were inside and Tony had closed the door after me Jack spoke for the first time. 'Take a seat, Alex.'

From this instruction I divined it was Jack who really wanted this conversation as he had now taken charge of the proceedings. We sat down round a wooden table.

Jack was clean-shaven and had short dark hair that matched his black clothes perfectly. His eyes had disconcertingly long and dark eyelashes that gave the impression he'd put mascara on them and this made him rather attractive. His expression was a troubled one.

'Alex, I – we…' He looked at Tony with a conspiratorial glance. 'We are somewhat concerned with the influence you're having on our congregation. When you first came to the church we were quite happy for you to join it despite your… apostasy.'

I raised my hand as an indication I was about to object to this word when Jack raised his hand even higher, and with the addition of closed eyes so I knew I had to wait until he had finished.

'I know how keen you are to explain your position *exactly* but what I want to discuss is much bigger than mere semantics. As I was saying, your lack of belief in an Almighty God was of some concern to us but we felt, with time, you might come round to see the error of your ways.'

This immediately forced my hand up a second time but Jack repeated his motions and I felt it was prudent to remain quiet for the time being until Jack had said his piece.

'We accepted your argument that people who belong to a church live longer than atheists and therefore it made sense to you – an atheist – to join a church to benefit from whatever "psychological" thing it might be that provided this protection.'

He pronounced, 'psychological' with a tone that suggested he was talking about snake oil.

'We're a loving and generous congregation here so we feel if anyone wishes to belong to our flock, for whatever reason, we are duty-bound... No, that's too unfeeling. We are *glad* that they wish to belong to our congregation.'

I looked at Tony and he nodded his approval at the beneficence of his flock. This time I spoke without indicating my intention: 'I did mention this right from the start that I'd looked at the data and—'

'Yes, yes, I understand all this and like I say, we had no qualms about welcoming you to our flock.' Jack then looked me straight in the eye and composed himself to reveal his true thoughts.

'My reservation now is that you have realized the great value of belonging to our church these past two years and have been evangelical about it to such an extent that you have collected quite a number of new members to our flock.'

I glanced at Tony again who looked slightly bemused at the conversation as if he were listening to two Nobel-winning mathematicians discussing Fermat's last theorem and he had never progressed beyond an O-level in the subject. I then looked back at Jack, whose young forehead was creased with a severe line of doubt.

'I thought you'd welcome a new influx of people to your congregation,' I said.

'Oh we do. Of course, every church rejoices in new members coming to the mission – especially when congregation numbers are falling across the UK. But the important word here is *mission*. As a church, we have a mission to spread the word of God and we' – he looked at Tony for support – 'hope that all new members of the flock will share that mission.'

'Are you saying we're not welcome anymore?'

'I don't mean anything of the sort, Alex, I'm merely pointing out that the twenty-four new members of our flock that you have introduced are also non-believers and we're concerned about what sort of... effect that might have on our true believers.'

The emphasis he'd placed on the word 'true' left no room for doubt: we were interlopers gate-crashing his private party.

'But we don't talk about our non-belief at all when we're involved in any of the church activities.'

'And you don't express any support for the Almighty either, that's what I'm talking about. Some members of our congregation have started to mention to me their unease at the number of people coming to church to simply extend their lives without acknowledging the existence of God.'

'Surely we're an asset to the church. We can be the modern upgrade to the church: the thinking woman's face of worship...'

As soon as I'd said the sentence I realized my mistake. Jack sat back in his chair and looked at me with open hostility. I glanced at Tony and even he had grasped the issues at stake and looked at me with pity.

'"Thinking woman's face of worship"? This is exactly the attitude I'm talking about, Alexandra. My congregation can sense your... unspoken disapproval—'

'No! I absolutely refute that allegation! You are perfectly entitled to your beliefs and I respect those beliefs. Why do you think I'm here? I approve and endorse your aims.'

'We're not children, Alexandra, requiring your approval or oversight of our actions. We've had two thousand years to grow up and learn what is right and wrong.'

There was a silence for several seconds as we looked at each other, marshalling our thoughts. Eventually, Jack broke the tension.

'The church council have had a discussion about it and the consensus is that the time has come... for a decision.'

Jack monitored my expression as he prepared to announce the decision. He continued.

'We would respectfully ask that you didn't attend the church when the activities involved worship.'

'Oh, I see. But most of the activities of a church involve worship in some way. How are you going to differentiate between the activities and thus decide which ones we can and can't attend?'

Tony volunteered information that I suppose he thought was being helpful to me: 'We'll have a look at the timetable and let you know which ones we think you'll be able to attend.' Then he smiled immediately afterwards.

I looked at Tony with a thoughtful expression and then at Jack, who seemed to be waiting for a reaction.

'Oh dear,' I said.

Jack raised an eyebrow and asked, 'Will that be a problem?'

'I think it might be. You see in the reports I read that analysed the data it conjectured that the beneficial effect of belonging to a congregation was the inclusiveness of the tribe. It's the sense of belonging that engenders the feeling of wellbeing. The activities themselves are largely irrelevant but it's the overall impact of sharing time together with welcoming people in a community that holds the key.

'If you start to exclude us from some of the activities, that in itself will negate the beneficial effect we might receive from attending those activities that you do allow us to attend. We will feel excluded and that is the cancer that eats into lonely people.'

Jack looked puzzled and annoyed. 'I didn't really follow all of that, Alexandra, but it sounds as if you're not happy with our decision.'

'I have to be honest with you Jack and tell you that, no, I'm not happy about your suggestion. I can see your point of view but I shall have to have a discussion with my fellow worshippers and see what they think about it.'

*

And so it was that three days later, twenty-five of us crowded into the upstairs meeting room in The Crown, the village pub on the hill, and discussed the problem. I made the case for our group:

'The data is clear, we have to feel part of the community, or there's no point in belonging to the church.'

'Can they decide just like that to exclude us?' This came from Matty, a dour woman who was so thin she looked like a cadaver.

'I'm afraid they can,' I said. 'It's their church and like a private club, they can eject members.'

'It's like we're being excommunicated!' cried Mary, a highly-strung bespectacled librarian, from the middle of the group.

'Don't be daft, Mary, we're non-believers, you can't excommunicate a non-believer,' said Jo scratching her unshaven armpit with one hand while vaping with the other. The denim dungarees she wore without a top allowed her easy access to the armpit.

Mary responded: 'That depends on your definition of "excommunicate"; if you define it as—'

'Oh, let's not get into semantics now,' said Jo.

'But that's what religion is!' shouted Cat, a retired data analyst.

The group descended into squabbling until a powerful voice cut through the noise.

'We should start our own church!'

The room fell silent. Everyone looked at the speaker, a blond-haired woman. She was the undisputed intellectual leader of our group and had studied the longevity data more than anyone.

'What do you mean, Virginia?' Mary asked.

Virginia stood up and turned to address the group. Her Geordie accent had a lovely sing-song quality but her voice was resolute and firm.

'We have fundamentally conflicting beliefs: they believe in God, we don't. We believe in Data, they don't. I canna see how our differences can be reconciled in the one church. We should break away and form our own church – the Church of Data.'

After some silence Jude, a gender-fluid coder, piped up: 'You do realize what you're suggesting, don't you, Virginia?'

Virginia nodded. 'A formal split between Believers in God and Believers in Data.'

A loud hubbub broke out in the group until I shouted above it: 'A schism in the church! That will cause trouble.'

In a voice burning with passion and defiance Paula called out, 'They can cause all the trouble they want for us but they won't stop our movement or our commitment for we have Data on our side!'

A Miracle in Raggio

Marco stood back from the gleaming Carrara marble he'd been working on. His cramped fingers were bleeding from the countless minor grazes he'd made against the emery sandpaper he'd been using to burnish the stone. His powerful arms ached from the many hours of applying pressure with them. The afternoon light coming through the windows of his extensive studio suddenly diminished in intensity as the sun disappeared behind a bank of white clouds, but it was still bright enough to allow him to inspect the sculpture in all its fine detail. He was covered from head to foot in the fine white powder of the marble and as he stood motionless to admire the statue he could have been carved out of stone himself.

One of my best pieces, he reflected.

The statue was of Hades ravishing the protesting figure of Persephone. Where Hades had hold of the flesh on Persephone's leg the flesh bulged around his fingers in an exact representation of how it would happen in real life (the original model and her bruised leg could testify to how this accuracy was achieved). Veins on the forearm of Hades stood out with such realism that if anyone were to touch them they would swear they could feel a pulse.

None of Marco's assistants were involved in this final task of polishing. It needed a master's eye to inspect every inch of an artwork before it could be deemed finished. As Marco's critical gaze travelled to the base of the statue his eye caught the pool of urine on the floor mirroring the sculpture – such was the concentration he brought to this task that for the duration of it he was oblivious to his bodily needs. Elsewhere in the studio his assistants were getting on with their regular duties – mixing pigments or pin-pricking cartoon outlines to prepare the image for transfer onto primed canvases or wooden boards, but whenever they could they would always take the opportunity to observe him at work. His total attention on the sculpture was something to behold and the assistants talked about it amongst themselves with awe. It was as if he were possessed by a magic spell, and he was seeing visions that others could not even begin to imagine. None dare disturb him when he was in this state.

Just at that moment, Giuseppe burst into the studio. He was a bald, fat man dressed in the fine clothes of a merchant. His pudgy, gold-ringed fingers carried a rolled up parchment trailing a scarlet ribbon encrusted with lumps of wax and he waved it about his head excitedly like some trophy.

'Marco! Marco! I have news!' he cried breathlessly, his face beading with sweat from his exertions and from the warmth of the day.

The assistants stopped what they were doing and threw alarmed looks at Giuseppe. Marco was still studying the marble in deep meditation and it took him a while to acknowledge that someone was shouting his name. He turned to look at Giuseppe, who, having realized his mistake in interrupting the master at work, waited for the onslaught of foul language (and possible physical blows) that was sure to come from Marco's infamous temper. It was rumoured that he had once killed a rival in another city during an argument over aesthetics but no one had any proof of this.

The gods, however, must have looked kindly on Giuseppe this day (or his timing was perfect) because there came no violent outburst of any kind from Marco.

He said, 'You come at a good time, Giuseppe, the Persephone sculpture is finished. You have the rare privilege of being the first person from the public to see it. Why don't you take a closer look?' Marco stepped to one side to allow Giuseppe a better view.

Giuseppe focused on the sculpture. With immaculate timing, the sun appeared from behind the clouds and raised the general ambient light level in the studio to its maximum. It gave the polished stone a divine, luminous look as the carved figures glistened seductively. His exuberance on entering the studio was instantly transformed into an intense stillness of concentration. Slowly he drank in the exquisite detail of the stone – the folds of cloth, the flowing locks of hair, the ripples of muscle, the pert breast of Persephone and the bud of her nipple... He approached nearer, looked closer (but didn't dare touch), disbelieving the evidence of his eyes.

'Marco... what have you created? It's as if you have breathed life into dead marble.'

Marco remained silent. He was his own fiercest critic and praise had no visible effect on him. This was often interpreted as arrogance by his rivals but when praise was offered (as it invariably was) he was secretly pleased that people recognized his genius.

After several minutes of silent admiration of the masterwork, Giuseppe's reverie was broken by the impatient voice of Marco.

'So, what is this news you bring me, my fat friend?'

Giuseppe snapped out of the spell induced by the statue.

'News? Oh, yes! Great news! Look at this letter – it is from the emissary of the Pope himself. The Pope, Marco!'

Marco took the proffered manuscript and as he did so the escaping marble dust from his powerful hand appeared to make the paper smoke. Whilst he silently read it, Giuseppe summarized the content of it aloud for the benefit of the curious assistants who were now crowded round the two of them.

'The Pope wants you to complete a commission. He requests that you attend an audience next month in Rome so he can describe his specific requirements. It is a great honour, Marco. Your genius has been acknowledged by none other than the greatest patron in the land.'

Marco studied the parchment. It was true; the Pope wanted him for a commission. He sensed that his time had come – and deservedly so, for he knew he was destined for great things. Gifted artists like him recognized their rightful place in history.

'And no doubt as my biggest patron to date you will want to attend too?'

Giuseppe blushed and feigned humility. 'I only ask that you mention my name. I would be honoured to be recognized as someone who helped you along your journey to immortal fame.'

A spontaneous applause erupted from the devoted assistants.

'Bravo, Marco!' they shouted. 'Bravo!'

Marco acknowledged the compliment without any hint of emotion.

*

Marco heard his name being called out – it echoed around the cavernous church and the vaulted ceiling. He left the hard bench he was sitting on and made his way along the patterned marble floor of the hall to the sunlit area of the room where the Pope sat on his ornate throne. His simple but magnificent costume was made from the finest and rarest materials his Portuguese tailors could lay their hands on.

Marco genuflected in front of Pope Boniface X and waited to be spoken to.

'Marco Barberini, your reputation precedes you. I welcome you to my house.'

'No reputation is greater than yours, Your Holiness. How may I serve your divine work on this earth?' Marco spoke his practised lines exactly as instructed.

'They tell me you can breathe life into stone and make paint sing. I require a mural for a new church. Is this something you can imagine yourself undertaking?'

Marco studied the opulent accessories of the Pope – the exquisite red silk slippers, the gilded chair, the giant magenta ruby in his curved staff – such items don't come cheap. *And nor does Marco*, he thought.

'It would be a blessing to undertake God's work and I pray that my skills will be worthy of your honour.'

'Excellent. I am pleased that you have accepted my commission. David, my assistant here' – without looking away from Marco, he indicated with his waving hand a handsome young man with lustrous black hair and such a heavy beard growth that his shaved chin had a dark blue sheen – 'will take care of all your needs and show you the Church of Assisi. I bid you farewell and bestow the blessing of Christ upon you.'

Marco stepped forward as he had been briefed to do by the advisors in the church and bowed his head. Pope Boniface X placed his hand on the top of Marco's head and murmured a short prayer before removing it. Wordlessly, Marco backed away, turned and accompanied David to a small antechamber adjoining the great hall. Upon seeing him leave, a secretary sitting at a desk in a recess of the great hall immediately called out a name from a list and a dark-skinned dignitary in brightly coloured flowing robes rose from the hard bench where Marco had recently sat.

*

David, now wearing a red silk cap, sat behind a wooden desk while Marco stood in front of it. David went through the conditions of the commission and explained the purpose of it. 'His Holy Father has a problem with some of his flock,' he said. 'The Raggio part of the city has not yet learned the lesson of charity. Their contributions to the Holy See are pitiful when compared with the contributions he receives from other parts of his flock.

'In Raggio is the newly built Church of St Assisi. It is in need of a mural and His Holy Father wishes it to instruct the worshippers on how to fully honour the work of the Church by being unstinting in their alms. They need to be shown what true charity is and why they should give up all they have for the Holy See. This is why the Holy Father seeks your talents.'

His dark, almost feminine eyes gazed languorously at Marco as he invited questions. Marco only had one: 'When can I see the church?'

Later, Marco, David and the accompanying notary walked through the city towards the Church of Assisi. Just as Marco had expected, the terms of the commission were hugely favourable to his bank account and the stipulated time scale gave him enough time to create something unforgettable, although anyone who commissioned a piece from Marco Barberini knew not to expect dates and times to be honoured when it conflicted with magnificence and perfection.

A Swiss Guardsman preceded them on their journey and cleared the way of beggars and children, of which there were many, by prodding them with his staff if they didn't move out of the way fast enough. As they neared the church they passed a couple of beggars who painted a picture of extremes. One was an old man who was blind and missing his legs. He was pitifully thin and terrible sores on his leg stumps oozed a yellow pus. The stink coming from him was unmissable, even in a street filled with fresh excrement. His companion was a small, dirty child who stood beside him and implored passers-by for alms with outstretched hands. Her short black hair framed her heart-shaped face and her eyes were dramatically lined with unusually long eyelashes. Her full lips were shaped like an archer's bow and her delicate bone structure conformed to all the accepted notions of what constituted classical beauty in a female form at that time.

Marco immediately stopped and got out his sketchbook to do a lightning-quick drawing of the child – the pathos of her was heartbreaking. On seeing Marco take an interest in her, the girl put more emotion into her begging. This excited Marco even more but when the girl realized he only wanted to draw her and not give her anything she lowered her arms and started to approach the other members of the group. Marco put down his sketchpad and fished out his leather purse from his tunic. He took out a gold coin and showed it to the girl, who immediately reached out for it with a look of amazement. Marco pulled the coin away and called David over and told him to hold the coin just out of reach of the girl, which he grudgingly did. Marco then picked up his sketchpad again and began to draw with ferocious intensity.

When he had finished drawing he took the gold coin from David and returned it to his purse. The child gave a wail of such despair that it made Marco stop and look at her with anger. He then noticed the disapproving looks of the peasants who had gathered to watch the brief moment of spectacle, so Marco opened his purse again and produced a copper coin to give to her. The girl stopped wailing but her expression was a confused one of gratitude and disappointment. Marco chuckled at the comedy of her plight.

On his frequent visits to other cities Marco was used to seeing beggars in the streets but the Raggio district he was now in had an overabundance of them and their extreme poverty was unusual to see. No wonder their contributions to the Church were so derisory – they needed every penny for themselves.

As they rounded a corner in the road the recently built Church of Assisi appeared out of the slums before them. It was a magnificent building, pharaonic in concept. It was already surrounded by a ramshackle array of encampments and market stalls attended by unsavoury-looking characters but Marco's eyes were inescapably drawn towards the towering church – it did indeed inspire the glory of God as he looked on it.

Inside the church, David didn't need to point out where the intended mural was supposed to go; Marco immediately recognized the space for its potential. He stood in front of the huge expanse of wall and as the light from a nearby tracery window illuminated the white plaster his fabulous mind set to work visualizing possible stories and compositions then blocking them in with shapes and colours…

*

Over two years later, the Pope's caravan made its way to the church for the official viewing. It consisted of nearly a hundred people. Six burly men dressed in white robes were carrying the Pope himself in his gilded sedan chair. In front of him walked a group of high-ranking officials who were in turn preceded by a scarlet banner held high by two Swiss Guardsmen that proclaimed the divinity of the Pope. Also in the human train were secretaries, notaries and cardinals, who all fanned their faces to alleviate the heat and stink surrounding them. Huge crowds of people lined the streets to cheer him on and admire the display of gold, silk and ivory – never in their lives had they seen such wealth and pomp and they welcomed the rare moment of entertainment as an escape from their ceaseless daily struggle for survival.

Arriving at the church, the Pope's sedan was lowered to the ground and he led the way into the cooler air of the interior followed by all the officials and visiting dignitaries. They assembled in front of a huge dung-coloured sheet of cloth.

From the beginning, Marco had instructed his assistants to hide the artwork behind this sheet. Even during the painting of the mural only Marco, his assistants and David were allowed to view it. It was only the regular ecstatic reports of progress from David to the Holy See that kept everyone happy and well away from the church. Such was Marco's reputation for being temperamental about work in progress that no one dare ask to look at what was being created aside from a few cartoons and sketches.

A big reveal had been planned. Part of Marco's success as an artist was down to his showmanship as well as his undeniable genius with paint and stone. When everyone was gathered and hushed, Marco positioned himself at one side of the huge curtain near the release mechanism. The mechanism was his invention and allowed the sheet to drop vertically as one piece rather than swing from the side in an untidy movement. The moment of disrobing had arrived. Marco's voice boomed in the vast space:

'My Holy Father, as I worked on this mural I felt the breath of God flow through me and I copied the vision He had given to me onto the wall of your church. I pray that my hands have faithfully reproduced what He described to me.'

Finally the rope was released and the cloth descended to the ground with all the majesty that gravity could afford. The effect was like a rough dress slipping off a beautiful woman and the response from the assembled crowd was equally dramatic. An involuntary gasp escaped the lips of onlookers as they first took in the vibrant colours of the masterpiece then silence descended as each person studied the many elements of the mural.

The dominant image of the entire piece was an angel. She stood facing the viewer and her arms were raised above her head as if in supplication. Her beautiful heart-shaped face had an impassive expression but the most shocking aspect of her was her eyes – they looked directly out at the viewer. It was unsettling to be looked at so intensely by this unsmiling angel; it was as if she looked deep into your soul and made you think absolutely nothing could be hidden from her gaze.

Some of the party were so overwhelmed by the exquisite detail and realism in the picture that they fell to their knees in devout submission before they had even had time to look at the mural properly. Tears of ecstasy began to swim in the eyes of some of the more pious cardinals. The quality of workmanship was undeniable. It was a triumph of coloured shit over reality – like God breathing life into clay.

The crowd continued to look on in stunned silence until someone said aloud, 'It's the girl! It's the beggar girl outside.'

At that, murmurs of discussion rippled through the crowd. The Pope looked bemused. A cardinal at his side leaned over to him and explained what the others had noticed. Pope Boniface X was curious. 'A beggar girl, you say? Is she outside now? Bring her here, let me see the likeness.'

Word was passed on and two Swiss Guards accompanied the man who had first voiced his recognition of the girl as he was dispatched to bring her to the Pope. While they waited for their return the crowd became animated and more vocal in their comments. Looked at closely, the deceptively simple composition revealed a world of many layers filled with allegorical figures and symbols. Many high-ranking officials eagerly looked for other details in the mural that might hide secret messages or reveal familiar faces to them.

Eventually the guards returned escorting the terrified little girl between them. The man who identified her walked at a discreet distance behind them, unsure of what he had just precipitated. The dignitaries parted like the Red Sea as the girl and guards walked through the church to where the Pope was standing. When the girl stood in front of the Pope, Marco noticed that she had grown little over the time from when he had first sketched her. The Pope observed her closely. The resemblance to the angel in the mural was unmistakable. Then he had an idea.

'What is your name, child?' asked the Pope.

In a tiny voice she answered, 'They call me Little Feet.'

'Little Feet, go and stand in front of the mural and raise your arms in the air as the angel does in the picture.'

The girl turned around and for the first time saw the mural with the angel. She nearly fainted with the shock of recognition. It was like looking into a mirror. Then a look of utter bewilderment filled her eyes – here she was, a nobody, immortalized for all time in a work of sublime beauty. She took small steps towards it. At the base of the wall she stopped, turned and faced the crowd. Slowly she raised her arms in supplication, echoing the pose of the angel above her. Hundreds of well-fed faces studied her in minute detail. Silence descended on the crowd once again. It was as if the imperious angel above her was the heavenly vision of redemption and the diminutive, dirty human specimen below was the vision of a corrupted soul before God finds it.

The effect was spellbinding. A collective moan of pleasure reverberated through the vaulted space of the church as if the congregation had all shared a vision of religious ecstasy.

The Pope could be seen mouthing an inaudible prayer. Then he said aloud for all to hear, 'This girl begs no more.'

Marco, standing close by the girl, inwardly rejoiced; from a heart of stone he had managed to squeeze out a single drop of blood – his towering genius had performed a miracle, right here in Raggio. His talent would be admired and remembered for as long as civilization persisted.

My best piece of work by far, he thought.

Bloom Boom

It was a *crump* sound, like something imploding. The vibrations through the floor and air made it obvious though that this was an explosion.

What Asif experienced next was the animal fear of fire – uncontrollable, feral, ancient. He felt the urge to run. He could feel a rising panic in his gut.

Asif was in his flower shop serving a customer, a middle-aged woman dressed in clothes that were too young for her. They looked at each other over the counter with frightened eyes.

'What was that?' asked the woman, already knowing the answer.

They both went to the window, the transaction forgotten. They could see down the street and the first frantic movements of panicked pedestrians. Then they heard the screams.

That was yesterday. Asif was still in a mild state of shock. What were the chances – a suicide bomber in his neighbourhood? Twelve people killed so far, dozens in hospital. The world media were camped outside the targeted building – a railway station, some two hundred metres down the street from his shop. It was unreal, like a Hollywood film.

Trade in his shop had slowed to a trickle. The only transactions going on were conversations with regular customers who used familiar clichés snatched from the media as their coinage. But Asif had an idea.

Ordinarily, such an idea would be a cause for him to celebrate but in this context it troubled him, and his conscience wrestled with it.

It was a short contest. Within fifteen minutes he was on the phone to his wholesaler.

'Josh, hi, it's Asif. I'd like to put in an order.'

'Asif, mate, your shop has been on the news! I caught a glimpse of it when they were trying to fill ten minutes of their twenty-four hour rolling news coverage. Are you and your family okay?'

'Yes, we're all okay. It's a circus round here, though, a bloody circus.'

'Did you see him, you know, the bomber?'

'Well, he didn't come into the shop to buy some flowers beforehand if that's what you mean. I heard it though, a loud bang.'

'Man, it must have been such a shock. Listen, I'm glad to hear you're okay, mate. These terrorists are the scum of the earth.'

'Thanks, Josh. So anyway… I need to get back into the shop to handle all the journalists who keep coming in and asking if I sell any fags…'

'Oh yeah, you wanted to order some more flowers.'

'I… I don't want you to think bad of me, Josh, but I remember seeing all those news stories of previous bombings. Within days they're laying flowers at the site of the bombing – hundreds of bunches. As I'm so near the site I reckon there's gonna be a demand for them.'

'Yeah, yeah, I seen that on the telly too. Hey, if people wanna lay flowers who are we to stop them? It's a free country, right, despite what the terrorists are trying to do to us?'

'That's right, that's what the politicians tell us – "don't let the terrorists interfere with our way of life, business as usual" and all that, so I know it's shocking and all but I don't want to miss an opportunity.'

'Nor me, mate. What flowers do you want and what quantity?'

'Can I have four times my usual order? No, wait – make it five. I'll see how demand goes and I'll be in touch again if it goes mental. Could well be I'll need more than that.'

'You got it, mate. I'll sort that lot out for you now. I'll speak to you later.'

Asif put his mobile phone away in his pocket. He was still troubled by the idea of making money out of the atrocity. It could be a lot of money though if he sold as many flowers as he anticipated. With the profits he could afford that new garden furniture he wanted. Shit! What was he thinking? People had died! Women and children!

He absent-mindedly picked up a newspaper and flicked through it in an agitated fashion. One of the articles was about the Prime Minister having to fly back to England from Saudi Arabia, where she was selling arms. Asif wasn't that sophisticated but even he could see the hypocrisy of the situation. No, he wasn't being so bad; at least he was just selling flowers to locals, not bullets and bombs to foreigners.

With that he went back into the shop, where his wife was talking to several journalists. Asif went behind the counter and took out from underneath it a small card with a printed flowery border. He got hold of the black Sharpie pen near the till and wrote on the card. He then went to the flower display and took out a bunch of carnations mixed with alstroemerias, gerberas and snapdragons. They were tied at the bottom by a pink satin ribbon. He tucked the corner of the card behind the band of pink ribbon and then said loudly to his wife, 'I'm just going to lay some flowers for the victims.' And with that he opened the clanging door of the shop and went out.

Near the site of the bombing he spoke to one of the policemen standing on the other side of the police tape.

A few words were exchanged and the policeman took the bunch of flowers, looked around to see where he could place them so they wouldn't be in the way of the forensic team. He found a suitable spot and the first bunch of flowers were laid.

The television news crews at the site noticed the gesture. Lenses panned and tilted onto the bunch of flowers. Powerful zoom lenses resolved the message in high definition.

The card read: 'I'm so sorry'.

Onlookers noticed the interest of the media at this solemn gesture. They unconsciously looked around to see where Asif had got his flowers.

It's Only Natural

The coffee I'd drunk earlier from my flask during our rest stop was now demanding an exit from my bladder. As we were in the centre of the most popular tourist attraction in the Lake District and it was summer I was confident there would be a public toilet open somewhere.

'I need the toilet,' I said to my wife, Katie.

'There's a sign for one,' she replied, pointing to some street furniture. 'I'll be in this shop when you've finished.'

I followed the sign to a stone building tucked behind the façade of the street. The entrance to the toilet had a turnstile. A sign told me the fee to enter was 50p and that a camera was monitoring my behaviour should I try any funny business (this last part wasn't spelled out but was implied by the mention of the camera).

Fifty pence! was my thought as I read this, and a red mist descended over me. Without another thought I moved a couple of steps to the side of the entrance and fiddled with the fly of my shorts. Once my penis was out I let a generous stream of hot piss cascade onto the wall of the building. Behind me I heard a passer-by tut loudly. The piss ran down the wall and onto the pavement between my feet before meandering towards the gutter. Another female voice behind me said, 'That's disgraceful!' then another younger male voice said, 'Do you need some change, mate?'

As I was emptying my bladder, I could see out of the corner of my eye a traffic warden approaching the toilet entrance and when he caught sight of me he stopped and challenged me: 'What do you think you're doing?'

'I'm having a piss,' I responded.

'I can see that but it's illegal and you can be fined for doing it in the street.'

'Well, I was desperate and there was nowhere to go.'

'What're you talking about? There's a toilet right here!'

I looked where he was pointing and said, 'You want me to piss on the turnstile?'

His face reddened at that and he felt for his walkie-talkie. 'Right, I'm calling the police,' and he barked some kind of code into his device and gave his location along with a description of a 'single middle-aged male'.

A policeman was on the scene remarkably quickly and the warden explained to him my offence. I had by this time finished my piss and put away my penis. A puddle of urine however, remained on the pavement. The policeman looked at the puddle and said to me, 'Did you do this?'

I replied, 'I think there was a dog that passed by recently so I can't be absolutely sure if I did it or not.'

The policeman's neutral expression changed into one of mild concentration. I continued: 'I suppose you could take a sample and have it sent to the lab. DNA analysis should be able to detect whether it's the dog's or mine. That's probably a lot of expense and trouble though for such a small thing as a puddle of piss.'

By this time the traffic warden was anxious to relieve himself and he said to the policeman, 'I have to go to the toilet. I won't be long though,' and he produced a pass that he waved in front of a sensor that activated the turnstile.

'Hey,' I shouted, 'it's fifty pence to enter.' The traffic warden threw me a look that was filthier than a motorway service station toilet on a Sunday afternoon during a Bank Holiday weekend and disappeared through the turnstile.

The policeman interrogated me again: 'Didn't you have the correct change?'

'Change?' I asked. 'I wanted to relieve myself, not buy a souvenir.'

'So you did relieve yourself out here and not inside the toilet?'

By this time a small crowd had gathered around us and one or two Chinese tourists were taking photographs. Presumably, they thought this was a typical English occurrence during a busy summer.

'Yes, I did. I also breathe out here to relieve myself of carbon dioxide poisoning. As yet, they haven't started charging for that bodily function.'

The policeman looked unmoved and said, 'Look, we can't have everybody relieving themselves in the street, it's unhygienic.'

'Well, in that case, perhaps they should provide some toilets that everybody can use.'

Some of the crowd had been standing around long enough to follow the argument and joined in. 'Yeah, what if you haven't got fifty pee?' a youth with a skateboard said.

The policeman looked around the crowd to divine its mood rather than try to identify the person who made the comment. On ascertaining that the crowd was still non-threatening he continued his questioning of me.

'I'm going to issue you with a fixed penalty notice.'

'What? Where's your evidence?' I asked.

A smartly dressed middle-aged woman from the crowd heard this and said, 'I was a witness, officer, I saw him do it.'

In response a male youth shouted, 'I saw the whole thing too, but it was a dog that peed against the wall.'

Another youth shouted, 'Arrest the dog!' Then an old man grumbled aloud, 'The toilets should be free.'

This time the policeman looked more uncomfortable about the intent of the crowd but then the traffic warden emerged from the toilet and the policeman felt a bit more secure.

'Have you fined him?' asked the warden.

'Fine the dog!' the youth shouted again and some of the crowd started laughing. The warden looked about him with a scandalized expression. 'It's not funny,' he said sternly to the assembled crowd, 'this man exposed himself.'

'So did the dog!' the youth replied. Now laughter infected the crowd.

Just then my wife appeared by my side and grabbed my arm. 'David, why are you taking so long and what's going on here?'

The policeman looked at Katie and asked her, 'Are you related to this man?'

Katie replied, 'Yes, he's my husband. What's happened?'

'I have a report that he urinated in the street just now,' the policeman explained.

Katie looked at me with a sad expression and sighed. 'Not again.' She then looked at the policeman and said, 'I'm really sorry about this but I'm his carer as well as his wife and when he said he was going to the toilet I assumed he could just walk in and use the toilet.' She looked closely at the turnstile. 'I didn't realize he'd have to negotiate some kind of mechanism to enter.'

The policeman and the warden suddenly looked perplexed and the policeman started to put his book away. Katie continued: 'He's got mild dementia but can still function on a simple level like going to the toilet so I thought it would be okay to leave him for a couple of minutes.'

'I see,' said the policeman. 'In that case I'll let the incident pass. Perhaps in future though you could check the toilet entrance before you allow your husband out of your sight.'

The warden scrutinized my face with an aggressive expression of disbelief. I returned his stare and gave him a little wink. His face ricocheted between two expressions, fury and doubt, at a speed that made me think of a pinball machine with the ball caught between two bumpers.

'Come on, David,' said Katie as she pulled me by the arm, 'let's see what they've got in the gift shop.' She cast one last look at the policeman and mouthed 'Thank you' before we disappeared down the street and the crowd dispersed.

Once we were safely out of earshot of anyone Katie said to me: 'I think we should drop this charade at the toilets – it's getting too risky.'

'But I like putting one over on the officious bastards – seeing their faces when you mention you're my carer, it's hilarious. You could be right, though. For the sake of fifty pence it might not be worth the risk of getting a copper who's such a twat he'd still issue a ticket. Anyway, how did your shopping go?'

'Oh, it went well. I've picked up some nice expensive things and I kept well out of sight of the shop cameras. I reckon fifty quids' worth.'

As we walked we passed a large dog on the pavement curving its back in readiness to defecate. The well-dressed female owner stood next to it watching the procedure. She pulled a blue plastic bag out of her jacket pocket and slipped it over her hand.

Of Gods and Monsters

Charles passed me the hookah pipe and in the golden light of the setting sun I admired its beautifully grained and varnished walnut handle. I took a long pull on the mouthpiece and allowed the smoke to infuse my lungs – a warm, fluffy blanket wrapped itself around my brain. Not, I noticed, as fluffy as it had once been. It was all true what they said about habituation: my experiences told me each time I indulged in a drug session it was harder to achieve the previous high and I could never manage the levels of my very first experience with that particular drug. The metaphor of *chasing the dragon* encapsulated perfectly the futile journey you embark upon when consuming narcotics for pleasure.

I handed the pipe back to Charles sitting alongside me on the silk-covered sofa. His tanned, bespectacled face had an avuncular look that would not have been out of place in the Home Counties, where he would have likely been pictured as a science teacher of some sort at a grammar school.

Our surroundings were not the typical ones associated with opium dens; we were in a light and airy air-conditioned sitting room that could have been straight out of the pages of a *Beautiful House* type magazine. Bach's chorale prelude for organ played in the background, reproduced with effortless precision by a powerful Naim hi-fi system. The furniture and décor were imported from the best design houses in Italy. The luxury was perfectly in keeping with the status that Charles enjoyed as a world famous author of many science fiction novels, screenplays, and several important scientific papers.

Many of his seemingly improbable predictions from decades ago have come to fruition with a vengeance, surpassing even his fecund imagination. His extraordinary success has allowed him to live anywhere in the world, which is why I had to cross several oceans to be there.

I'd known Charles for most of my life, we were at boarding school together, and although my career as a political fixer looks tragic when compared with his, we never lost touch. Painful experiences shared with close friends during a traumatic education can forge bonds so powerful that they defy whatever life has to throw at them. When Charles started to enjoy his spectacular success he never distanced himself from me and never failed to invite me to his regular private parties on his secluded estate.

As usual, I was the first to arrive for his latest party so as we waited for the other specially selected guests to turn up we speculated on life.

'Tell me, Charles, do you think that one day virtual reality will be able to replicate these intimate parties you organize?'

Without any hesitation he answered: 'I'm certain of it. As technology improves and we discover more about how *qualia* is reproduced in the brain we'll be able to access the mechanisms and amplify them to unimaginable levels.'

'I'm not so sure,' I mused. 'I feel certain experiences are beyond the realm of the brain. When I'm in the middle of having sex, for example, I can't imagine anything rivalling that intensity. I'm sure people will miss the *animal* in it.'

'Think of the novelty element though, Jacob – that would more than compensate for any peripheral biological influence. And of course nothing is off limits; every fantasy will be available to you.'

His eyes shone. The idea had enormous appeal for him. Throughout his life he'd been careful (and successful) to conceal his peccadilloes from the gossip-hungry media. I supposed living in an underdeveloped country helped in that regard.

'I can see why that appeals to you – your fictional work tends to explore the extreme scenarios offered by a limitless universe. That freedom to explore, I guess, is how you come up with some of your best ideas. I mean, visualizing aliens that look like demons travelling across the vastness of space creating gardens of Eden everywhere they go and then eventually destroying the earth – it's mind-blowing stuff. And heretical.'

There was a pause as we absorbed the effects of the drug. Then I went on: 'Thinking about it, most of your fiction involves transition or transcendence of some kind – humanity on the edge of some profound change. So living on the edge of what society deems to be acceptable or unacceptable would make sense. How come you've never written about the possibilities of what virtual sex might offer?'

Charles looked slightly embarrassed by my comment and said, 'There's a lot of hysteria in the West about sex. I think it's a glitch in history. Ancient civilizations never had any qualms about it. I find it much easier to explore territory that lies beyond everyday human experience. The public don't mind so much if you abuse their gods, it's when you deal with issues that affect them in the real world that they are liable to get upset.

'But you're right, all the interesting things happen at the edges – evolution is always experimenting with the extremities of possibilities. There's eventually a tipping point, a change of direction.

'We even see this demonstrated in our own history. Think of a coup attempt in the middle ages. The pretender to the throne would have to make a decision about when and how to strike. That calculation must be fascinating to analyze. Don't forget, if all goes well, the pretender is installed on the throne and from then on history acknowledges him as a man of substance. If he fails, however... he's either imprisoned or executed as a traitor and largely forgotten by history as a hopeless tragic figure. He's the same man in both outcomes but fate will paint him in whatever colours it chooses.'

'And how do you think history will view you, Charles?'

'Do you mean my work or me as a man?'

'Don't they come as the same package?'

'Sometimes. But look at Caravaggio; the vast majority of people who admire his paintings have no conception of the violent murderer behind the masterpieces.'

I looked sideways at him. 'You haven't murdered someone have you, Charles, just to see what it was like?'

He returned my gaze and said, smiling, 'Of course – I regularly *kill my babies*. But you're not talking about the metaphorical, are you?' He looked into the middle distance and searched his thoughts before he said, 'I suppose if the opportunity arose in virtual reality, I would. I mean, what person could resist the temptation?'

This made me consider my own likelihood of crossing the line into murder. Some of my past experiences suggested it was entirely possible. I preferred to think about the imminent future, however, and I said, 'Fortunately, this evening will be full-on reality – sex, drugs and rock 'n' roll! And hopefully, without any killings.' I took the pipe again and sucked on it.

'Don't you find it strange,' I went on, 'how, despite our intellect, we're still tied to this primitive urge to fuck? It seems inescapable.'

'I haven't really given it much thought.'

I was shocked. 'Surely not, Charles. A man of your towering intellect and curiosity – I would have thought you of all people would analyze the nature of such a fundamental force in nature.'

Charles gave a little laugh. 'Sex is like Schrödinger's cat: if you try to analyze it while you're trying to experience it, one or the other must die; you can't do both.'

'Yes, I see your point but you must have some inkling of what goes through your mind when you have sex.'

He looked at me as if to check if there was some hidden motive behind the comment. I can only guess he didn't find any because he allowed himself to explore the phenomenon as any good scientist would.

'Can you elucidate with your own experiences and I'll see how they compare with mine?'

I laughed. 'I see what you did there. Okay, I'll be your lab rat.' I thought carefully for a minute then said, 'I've noticed my urges seem to have two states. Sometimes I'm in control of the urge and I can direct my pleasure – almost logically – towards a blissful release. The other state is where the urge controls me, and my personality becomes possessed by the all-consuming demand for gratification. In those moments I feel I'm prepared to do anything, commit any kind of violence to satisfy the demon within me. I suppose that all goes back to the evolutionary idea of fighting for the right to mate and explains why sex is inextricably linked with violence.' I became animated. 'Hey, now that I think about it, a lot of your characters are faced with forces they can't comprehend or control – an alien represents that fear, doesn't it? Is that how you feel about the sex drive?'

Charles smiled at me through a miasma of smoke. 'My, my, Jacob, where have you unearthed these insights?'

I smiled back at him. 'I can't help feeling, Charles, that you're similar to an accountant friend I once knew. In his professional life he had to deal with vast sums of money – hundreds of millions of dollars. He became inured to these fortunes and moving them around cyberspace from one account to another gave him a god-like power. So it was a bit of a shock – he told me – when he sometimes got home and found a bill waiting for him for $120. He was tempted to toss it aside; what's a paltry $120 when he was used to dealing with millions? But of course, he couldn't ignore it. For all his hubris, an unpaid bill could still mean a court appearance.

'It's just occurred to me. It's as if all your stories are about change. Irresistible forces, the religious imagery – these take place in the vastness of space, they expand outwards like the universe itself. But according to Einstein, if you travel fast enough and far enough you eventually end up from where you started in the universe so these concepts of yours all come back to where they started – the primitive forces within ourselves. I mean, look at you, you're a celebrity here, feted by politicians and academics; you've got a brilliant mind that can almost see into the future and yet you don't apply this ferocious analytical mind to your own sex drive. Maybe' – my eyes widened as an epiphany illuminated my thoughts – 'maybe your stories stem from this struggle!

You turn these monsters into gods as a means to own them.'

Charles responded to my enthusiasm and sat up before saying, 'That's a nice theory, Jacob. Seriously, I think it would work in a story. I'll file that if I may for future reference.'

He passed me the pipe and reached for a moleskin notebook lying on a little mahogany table at the side of the sofa. He was famous for these notebooks; the slightest interesting thought was recorded in them. These notes were like the ore from which he would later process and refine his exceptionally pure material. Using shorthand, he summarized the idea.

Just then Charles's servant came into the room. 'Everything is ready for the gathering tonight, master Charles. There is just the… main course to attend to.'

'Very good, Suranga. Please sort that out too. Go and fetch the young boys. Our guests will be arriving soon.'

Survivor Score

Philippa ran her forefinger around the deckle edge of the ivory-coloured invitation card. She liked the sensation of it. She also liked to look at the card – its printed gold edging, the coat of arms, and the black, hand written calligraphic inking of her name: *Philippa Jones.*

This was a proud day for her. After decades of work in the technology field her contribution was finally being recognized, even if belatedly. She took off her reading glasses, folded them and put them into her designer mostly foundation. When she was younger she had never clutch bag along with the card. She made a final check in the hall mirror. Her smart clothes were fashionable enough and there was only a hint of makeup on her face, really bothered with makeup and now, in her seventies, she wasn't about to change her ways no matter how grand the occasion. From the mirror stared back a face of confidence and health, grey hair carefully styled.

The reflection then revealed her husband Dominic walking down the stairs behind her. 'The car's here,' he said. He was dressed in a dark suit, white shirt and a paisley bowtie. 'And how fitting that you are to be recognized for helping to bring it here!' With a dramatic flourish he opened the front door for her.

'You wouldn't be making fun of me, would you, Dom?'

'Never! Seriously, you deserve the award, you earned it the hard way.'

They both made their way to the waiting car.

*

At the airport, a gleaming limousine was parked on the tarmac of the runway. Behind it was a black SUV with three men inside it. All were wearing dark suits and had earpieces. Surrounding the vehicles was a group of smartly dressed people waiting for an aeroplane to taxi to a stop a few hundred yards in front of them. When it did, a set of steps were wheeled up to the plane, a uniformed band struck up the 'Stars and Stripes' and a red carpet was rolled out.

Callum Brody was getting too hot in the SUV. He was bigger than the other two security men so he suffered more in the heat but less in the cold. 'I'll be glad when we can get going and turn on the aircon,' he moaned. He said this with a high-pitched voice which, when juxtaposed with his formidable stature, sounded faintly comical. But his most striking feature was his mouth. It lacked any discernible lips and appeared to be slightly pushed back into his face. The straight line of his mouth coupled with the skinfold lines emanating from the corners resembled one of the diagrams from that famous puzzle where two lines are of the same length but one of them looks longer because it has branching lines attached to either end whereas the other line has inward-facing arrows at either end. His mouth described the longer- looking line perfectly.

'Just think of the overtime,' said Brett fingering the scar on his face that constantly irritated him and which he stroked now out of habit. 'That should keep you cool.'

'Okay, stop fucking around now, the *package* is here,' said Denziger, who was sat in the controller's seat and scanned the tarmac for anything unusual. The other two adjusted their body postures to indicate they were on the case. Denziger brought the SUV to life.

The *package* was the US Secretary of State. He climbed into the limousine idling just in front of them and they waited for Randy Holdsworth, the limousine driver, to start up.

*

At a nearby hospital, an ambulance had its back doors open as it waited in a reserved area adjacent to some exit doors. A porter named Phil Dent pushed a wheeled stretcher carrying Tiffany Sparks through the doors, followed by Gayle Thornton dressed in the blue uniform of a palliative care nurse. Phil and Gayle positioned themselves at either end of the stretcher and prepared themselves for the lift.

'Are you okay with this – no bad back or anything?' asked Phil.

Gayle responded with: 'If I had to stop work every time I had a bad back, I'd never be here.'

'These staff cuts are getting ridiculous,' said Phil. 'It wouldn't surprise me if they expected only one of us to do this lifting job.'

'You're not wrong there. Either that or they'll expect us to try and involve members of the public to help out. Ready? One, two, three...' Together they hoisted the stretcher in one swift, well-practised movement.

Tiffany was awake and alert as the stretcher levitated. She was 16 years old and bald.

'You all right, Tiffany?' asked Gayle.

'I've had better rides,' said Tiffany. She was trying to be upbeat but it was all bluff; she felt lousy. 'I went to Alton Towers once with my school. It was a reward for being good all year.'

'Rather you than me,' said Gayle, 'I'm not a big fan of adventure rides.'

*

'Guys, the Google car is here!' shouted Matt. He was excitedly waiting by the front door of their student house. It wasn't the first time they'd ordered up a driverless car but the novelty still hadn't worn off. As he was studying pure mathematics and machine learning at the university, he understood the incredible calculations that were going on in the systems that allowed the car to navigate the busy streets all by itself. And he still marvelled at the reality of it.

The car came to a stop in front of the house. Matt's phone vibrated with a message. He looked at it, knowing it would be confirmation that his car had arrived.

Three young men emerged from the house, the last one closing the door and locking it. One of them flicked Matt on the shoulder with the back of his hand and said, 'How many times do you have to get excited over these things before they become just another piece of technology you use every day? Get in!'

The four of them climbed into the vehicle. Ben shouted: 'Let Matt direct the car, he thinks he's the captain of the star ship *Enterprise* whenever he does it.' In unison, the three students pointed at Matt and, impersonating one particular captain in the series, ordered: 'Engage!' The car pulled away smoothly, and effortlessly entered the traffic system.

*

The introduction of driverless vehicles had revolutionized traffic on the roads. Once all the vehicles became autonomous and talked to each other, road death figures plummeted. Traffic jams were a thing of the past as every vehicle knew what was happening on the length of road they were travelling on and could automatically adjust their speed to smooth out any bumpy fluctuations in traffic density that used to cause the phantom traffic jams of the past. And because there were fewer accidents (and no driver interference), the possibility of *rubbernecking* was also eliminated.

As the algorithms were being written for what to do in the eventuality of an accident, moral dilemmas had begun to emerge. In some scenarios, passenger deaths were envisaged – so the choice of which passengers to save and which to sacrifice was an available option. The likelihood of these choices actually being needed was infinitesimally small. However, once the mainstream media got hold of the information they overplayed the significance of the preferences and made the issue much bigger than it actually was.

What the public picked up on was the phrase 'Survivor Score' that the algorithms used. This used a simple analysis. How many individuals are involved in the collision? Then a calculation is made with the intention of choosing to preserve the greatest number of lives. If the algorithms have to choose between car A, containing four people, or car B, carrying only one person, the manoeuvres would favour car A since more lives would be saved.

But then someone in the security services had an idea. They knew that intelligent, well-read people were voluntarily carrying with them a tracking device that told the security services everything they needed to know about the owner – where they'd been, whom they'd called, which websites they'd looked at, etc. If the security forces chose to, they could even eavesdrop on conversations going on around the device through its built-in microphone. These devices were smartphones and the security forces constantly marvelled at how readily the public willingly embraced them. Now they saw a similar opportunity with Survival Score.

What the security forces did was to instruct the vehicle manufacturers to weight the Survival Score of certain people in the Establishment because they were indispensable to the running of the country. In the event of a catastrophic accident, this weighting would make the algorithm attempt to preserve the life of the important person over a less important one.

Initially, it was the manufacturers of luxury vehicles who were instructed to do this. But as soon as other members of the élite got wind of it they insisted that they had their own Survival Score weighted too. To be weighted correctly, the vehicle had to know who was riding in it and why they were important, so it made sense for the authorities to link up the smartphone technology with the operating system of the autonomous cars.

Before long, people were obsessed with their Survival Score and looked for ways to increase it. They did this by volunteering information about themselves on social media that demonstrated how valuable they were to society. The security forces couldn't believe their luck: by using the Score as a Trojan Horse, they had ushered in a totalitarian state completely unopposed.

People who wanted to volunteer information that increased their Survival Score were understandably disinclined to volunteer information that threatened to reduce it – so information such as criminal history, medical history, disabilities, etc was missing from the database. To compensate, the security services added this information covertly.

Ultimately, the Survival Score became as important to a person as their passport; without it they couldn't do anything or travel anywhere.

*

By the time all the concerned vehicles reached the bridge, the chain of events that would result in a crash was set in motion. The speed of the vehicles and their direction of travel meant that, by the laws of physics, some of them were going to suffer damage. *How much* damage was yet to be determined.

Matt and the other students were in high spirits and were playing a multiple-player game on their phones.

They would be the first to notice that something was wrong.

Dominic and Philippa in the light blue City Ford were totally unaware of what was about to take place. Their reflexes were too slow to notice the sudden change of direction that their car took in that initial moment. And anyway, Dominic was dozing.

The three dark-suited men in the black SUV *did* notice the impending crash. As security men, their reflexes were trained to sense anything out of the ordinary. As soon as they felt the slight shift in momentum, they all fell silent and became tense.

Tiffany and Gayle in the ambulance were as oblivious to what was happening as Dominic and Philippa. Gayle was busy checking a reading on a monitor above the head of young Tiffany.

Randy, the driver in the bullet-proof limousine, could see what was about to happen. The limousine still featured a steering wheel. Randy was the only one watching the road; but even as his hands began to rise from his lap to grasp the wheel, he knew that there was nothing he could do to avoid it.

The four students in the Google Car were the first to notice the start of the chain of events. They felt a jolt in the car's movement and then experienced a drunken swerving.

What happened next took just five seconds. But all decisions regarding the outcome of the crash had already been taken before the first collision.

Randy just managed to grip the wheel before the crash happened, but it was really only there for show. The car did have a manual override in case of emergencies; but the chances of something occurring where a human driver would need to take over from the onboard computer were so small as to be practically nonexistent. And in this instance the car had already decided what to do even before Randy had managed to touch the wheel.

So the accident about to happen between the limousine, SUV, City Ford, Ambulance and Google car was now a chess game.

As soon as the Google car gave a jolt in its movement, all the vehicles surrounding it knew there was a problem and they began their many calculations. But when they tried to talk to the problem car to assess its malfunction the car didn't send back the secret signal so they worked on the premise that its operating system was compromised. This meant the unthinkable had happened: a malicious hacker had managed to penetrate the defences and take control of the vehicle and override its safety protocols. This was bad news for the four students in the Google car as they were now considered perpetrating an act of terrorism and their combined Survival Scores were reduced to zero. Everyone in the car was considered expendable – collateral damage.

The first order of priority of the algorithms was to minimize property damage. The preferred evasion manoeuvres were designed to find the path of least destruction. If this calculation resulted in serious human injury or death then it crossed a threshold on the algorithm and a new set of calculations took place based on everyone's Survival Scores.

Dominic and Philippa were assessed. He was aged 73 and she was 71. Both were in good health and their insurance suggested they would live another sixteen years or so. He had a Score of 64 and she had one of 66 – a combined total of 130.

The two females in the ambulance were 16 and 38 – much younger than Dominic and Philippa – so their combined Survival Scores should have been way higher.

But the data showed Tiffany was being treated for leukaemia and the prognosis wasn't good. Her medical records showed that even with the best possible medical attention she had a life expectancy of nine months, so their combined Survival Scores were heavily discounted and nearly fell below the elderly couple.

The security men in the SUV numbered three, so their total would exceed Dominic and Philippa's. The fact that one of them had a criminal record for manslaughter would have counted heavily against him had it not been for the fact that all the men were designated as part of the cargo for the US Secretary of State, so they enjoyed privileged immunity from having their Survival Scores rated. The vehicle was automatically assigned secondary importance after the limousine.

The Google car that was being forced into the path of the limousine was controlled by an operator in another part of the world. It was being used as a weaponized drone. As much as the security forces tried to guard against this, it was inevitable that powerful technology would fall into the wrong hands at some point.

All the occupants of the vehicles were now helplessly in the control of the algorithm as it prepared to pronounce judgement on them during the crash.

The limousine adjusted its direction of travel slightly to improve its aim for the Google car. It even accelerated. The algorithm had taken into account the mass of all the vehicles involved and had concluded the best course of action was to ram the rogue car and use the greater mass of the limousine to plough a route in a line as straight as possible.

The four students managed a brief moment of horror before the seven-ton limousine piled into them like a wrecking ball. Matt and Ben, who were in the front seats, took the full force of the blow. The airbags made a brief appearance before they emulsified the flesh of the young men. All four students had their bodies compressed into unnatural shapes by the crushing force. None of them would survive the impact. Randy would suffer broken bones in both his legs and lacerations to his face caused by the airbag exploding from the steering wheel.

The accelerating limousine – with the Google car now impaled on its bonnet – smashed into the rear of Dominic and Philippa and sent them spinning into the path of the ambulance. When the ambulance hit the Ford it was sent skyward like a breaching whale and forced over the guard barrier of the bridge. It tumbled down into the river 30 feet below. Neither of the two females would survive the fall.

The dozing Dominic would die in his sleep; and Philippa, who was sending a text message at the time, would suffer whiplash injuries she would never fully recover from.

The only vehicle to escape any damage was the SUV following the limousine. It automatically switched on its hazard warning lights and issued a distress signal to the emergency services as it cruised to a standstill. All traffic on the bridge simultaneously came to a stop like a flock of birds reacting as one.

The US Secretary of State was uninjured apart from minor lacerations from the exploding airbags and flying glass (the shards were from the lead-crystal tumblers inside the car and not the windscreen, which was shatter-proof).

In another part of the world – thousands of kilometres away from the scene of devastation – screen-captured footage of the crash supplied by several of the cameras on the Google car was already being expertly edited into a prepared propaganda piece about the attack, complete with auto-tuned chanting and symbolic flag-waving, ready to upload to YouTube and feed the hunger of a vengeful audience.

The Business of War

Hordes of uniformed schoolchildren – some in black blazers, some in blue, some in grey – marched through the interconnecting aisles of the gift shop inspecting the bounty on offer with an excitement that bordered on the hysterical. Their anticipation had been building all afternoon during the march round the famous First World War battle site following knowledgeable tour guides who fired stories and facts at them throughout the field trip.

Several teachers accompanied the children into the shop and occasionally barked restraining orders at the known troublemakers in their charge.

Magdalena, the female store manager, and her two young assistants, also female, wore expressions of alarm at this mass invasion. They knew they would soon be overwhelmed at the tills by mobs of impatient kids clutching their gifts like weapons, and demanding service. They also knew from experience that replenishing the vanishing stock during the siege was going to be nearly impossible.

On the other side of a stout wooden door set in one of the walls of the shop, Victor was in his office. He was busy looking at a brochure for a new car, a two-litre Audi convertible. His current car, though perfectly usable, was two years old now, and he felt he deserved an upgrade. The shop had experienced a boom period last season and as Victor was a stakeholder in the business he could expect a financial bonus coming his way.

As he visualized himself driving the new convertible through a sunlit countryside with the sweet-smelling wind blowing through his ample blond hair, his desk telephone rang. Annoyed at being forced back to reality, he grudgingly picked up the receiver. It was a call from Magdalena, the store manager. 'Help!' was all that she barked into the mouthpiece before slamming the phone down.

Victor jumped up from his desk and rushed to open the door. What greeted him was a scene of carnage. There were more people in the shop than he believed it could possibly handle. He guessed that through some error in the booking system several school trips had arrived at the same time. The policy of the site was to stagger coach loads into manageable numbers by allocating specific time slots throughout the day. Even though the five-acre site could easily accommodate large numbers of visitors, the gift shop was the bottleneck.

Victor made a mental note to complain later to the ticket office at the entrance that they weren't doing their job properly. They should have realized the admission numbers were far too high. But that would have to wait. Right now, he was needed to take command.

Victor immediately signalled to Asil, the security man standing by the entrance to the shop, to close the doors and not allow any more people in until sufficient numbers had exited. A press of young bodies was already besieging Magdalena and the two girls on the tills.

Victor's first thought was, *God knows how much stock we are going to lose due to shoplifting*, but it was quickly followed by, *Still, the profits from today should more than make up for the losses.*

Victor went to the tills and took up position in the bagging area. He and Magdalena had a long-standing relationship in the shop and this was the accepted drill during an emergency. Magdalena was now free to manage the queue better and to fetch stock from the supply room. This system was holding up fairly well until one of the girls looked up from her till and threw a panic-stricken look at Victor. 'We're running out of change,' she said.

Merde! thought Victor. He nodded to the girl, looked for Magdalena, but she wasn't in the shop and must have gone into the storeroom. 'Do the best you can!' he said aloud and barged his way back to his office.

Once inside, he dived for the safe. Such was his adrenalin rush that he mistyped the security code for the safe and it refused to open. He tried again, this time forcing his fingers to slow down. The metal door clunked open, revealing its payload. Plastic bags of different denomination coins lay neatly packaged on a shelf, ready to be deployed. Victor simply scooped up what he could carry in his arms. Such was the emergency that he didn't even attempt to account for the cash he'd taken – he would try to work out the value later. Using his backside he closed the safe door, and headed out of the office again.

As he waded through the river of children, Victor stumbled against a schoolboy who was stooping to retrieve his dropped book of war poems, and a bag of coins slipped from the pile in his arms. As soon as it hit the floor a large child bullying his way through the aisle accidentally kicked it into a crowd of legs. Victor debated whether to stop and try to recover it there and then or to sacrifice it in order to speed up the rate of commerce at the tills. He didn't hesitate.

'Whoever brings me that bag of change can have a free gift!' he shouted at the gang of children nearest the bag. He then turned and fought his way back to the tills to the relief of his staff.

The cry from Victor had the desired effect and suddenly dozens of school children were looking at the floor. Lakshay was the nearest boy to the bag and saw it first. As he was short for his age he didn't have far to move to pick up the bag, and his coffee-coloured hand was onto it in a flash. His attempt to put the bag into his blazer pocket was observed by some bigger school boys flanking him and they shouted out, 'Laki's got it!'

A few minutes later, as Victor was bagging gifts near the till, a boy approached him. The boy was tall and had the build of a young athlete. His tie was loose and hanging at a drunken angle, as if he'd just come out of a rugby scrum. He held out the bag of change triumphantly in his white hand. 'Can I choose any gift I want?' he asked.

Slightly surprised at the reappearance of the lost bag, Victor took it, and the weight of it told him that something like 25% of the coins was missing.

'Thanks,' he said flatly.

He now had to make a delicate calculation. The bag had a value of five euros. With the coins pilfered from the bag it was more like four euros at the most. He didn't want to be out of pocket but the boy had made the effort to return the bag and was expecting his honesty to be rewarded. The till was short on change, though, so the remaining four euros in coins could help them avoid many minutes of lost trade, and how much was that worth? So, should he offer a prize worth more than the value contained in the bag?

'Choose anything up to five euros.'

The boy pulled a face but immediately disappeared to look for his prize. In less than a minute he was back waving a plastic model of a horse carrying King Richard III. Its price tag was €6.25. Victor, frowning, looked at the boy. His unblemished face was filled with the carelessness and bravado of youth; everything in life was still an adventure for him. A brief stand-off occurred during the locking of eyes but the boy refused to be intimidated and used pure hubris to stand his ground.

Victor, calculated that if he deducted the mark-up on the toy it would still be worth less than the five euros he'd allocated, so he nodded his assent and the boy whooped in triumph.

The struggle in the shop had lasted for an hour. There were big holes of empty shelves throughout the store and various leaflets promoting other excursions littered the floor.

Finally, Magdalena was able to turn the door sign to 'CLOSED' with a huge sigh of relief.

The two young assistants had already left the shop to go home, exhausted and demoralized, as had Asil, the security guard.

'Magdalena Futsch,' said Victor as he marched into his office, 'I need you in here now.'

She moved across the floor space and followed Victor into his office. Victor closed the door behind her and as soon as he did so Magdalena was onto him, pushing him against the wood. Her lips were clamped firmly on his mouth and her hand guided his hand onto her breast. Victor didn't need any encouragement with this manoeuvre, and his hand roved freely over her breasts, round her back and to her smooth, firm buttocks.

Using his tie, Magdalena pulled him towards the desk, where she then reclined onto her back, her buttocks pressing down on the open pages of the Audi brochure.

Just like the children in the shop earlier, they could hardly contain their excitement at the prospect of some real fun, and they pushed and pulled at various bits of anatomy and clothing with thoughtless abandon. Their frenzied coupling soon achieved an intense climax.

For several minutes they lay on the table panting and saying nothing. A pungent-smelling goo – a mixture of semen, vaginal fluid and early menstrual blood,

71

dripped from their bodies onto the desk, staining the pages of the car brochure.

As they both lay there in silence, Victor drifted into a fantasy about opening another gift shop somewhere, expanding his territory. Magdalena was deep in a reverie too – one that involved having children and nurturing them into fine young men who would one day go on to accomplish great things.

Marbles

'Is it in?'

'Yes, you can start lowering.'

Hector pushed the suspended sculpture of Aphrodite into the gaping maw of the van. Beads of sweat on his forehead sparkled like glass in the bright sunshine. His perspiration was largely due to the heat of the day rather than any physical exertion. He was using his considerable bulk to hold the sculpture in place.

Martin was operating the levers of the device he used to move large pieces around his yard – a crane system mounted on a wheeled platform. He checked that the sculpture was sufficiently over the floor of the van before expertly lowering it. He then joined Hector to give the sculpture a few more pushes so that it was completely inside the vehicle. He then undid the straps that held the sculpture to his crane device and helped Hector secure the sculpture in the van using the black nylon straps that were bolted evenly along the inside of it.

Once they were out of the vehicle, Martin backed his device away from it.

As Hector slid the side door of the van shut, Martin said, 'That's the hard work over and done with. Can I interest you in a celebratory glass of wine?'

Hector, dressed in a stripy short-sleeved shirt, Bermuda shorts and deck shoes, smiled at him from under a thick mop of salt-and-pepper hair and said, 'That would be more than welcome, thanks.'

The two men walked through the yard passing various bits of antique ironwork, wood and stone and past several secure sheds until they came to the little coach house at the entrance to the compound that Martin had for his office. Martin had a shock of unruly white hair and moved with a litheness that belied his advancing years.

The cosy office had a little fridge in the corner and Martin went to this to retrieve an unopened bottle of white wine.

'Are you okay with Chardonnay?'

'Right now I'd be okay with anything so long as it was cool and wet,' Hector replied.

Martin then went to the white porcelain sink and picked up two glasses from out of the drainer. He walked back to Hector and handed him a glass. He put his own glass on the desk next to him and unscrewed the top off the wine bottle. He offered the bottle to Hector first, who held his glass steady. The *glug-glug* sound of the wine as it poured out of the bottle was one of the finest pieces of music any art lover could ever wish to hear during a long hot summer.

'It's a pleasure doing business with you, Hector. To Aphrodite,' Martin said and the two men chinked glasses.

There was a pause as the two men took their time in savouring the wine.

'Where are you thinking of putting her?' Martin asked.

'I've got a spot next to my pond in the garden. There's a kind of harbour with an old rowing boat tied up there – she'll make a nice counterpoint as she watches over things.'

'Harbour? It sounds like quite a pond.'

'Okay, it's a large fishing pool – my garden is a couple of acres.' Hector glanced out of the open door. 'You've got some really nice pieces here.'

'Thanks. That's what comes from a lifetime of being in the antiques trade. By the way, are you going to be okay at the other end getting Aphrodite out?'

'Oh, I won't be manhandling her again, I've got a groundskeeper and two strapping sons at home.'

Martin nodded and drained his glass. He filled it again from the bottle. He waved the bottle at Hector in a questioning manner, who drained his own glass and held it out saying, 'I'll just have one more – don't want to risk harming my new acquisition by driving too fast, although two glasses of wine won't have any effect when poured into this frame.' He flicked his elbows out like a chicken to indicate his body mass index.

The afternoon was hot and still and the two men enjoyed the pleasure of it. Neither of them had any other pressing business that Sunday so Martin helped himself to the rest of the bottle as the conversation flowed as easily as the wine.

'So, you say you've spent a lifetime in the antiques business. How did you get into it?'

Martin smiled wryly and said, 'Oh, it's a long story.'

Hector waited but Martin didn't offer any more information. He prompted him: 'I like stories, and on a day like today I could probably stand a long one, too. I can see you appreciate good work. Did you go to art college?'

Martin studied him through watery eyes; the heat and alcohol were having an effect on him. 'I did, as it happens, but there was one particular incident that really got me interested in antiques.'

Again, Hector waited for more information but Martin was lost in a reverie and his eyes were looking into the middle distance.

'What was the incident?'

Martin suddenly snapped out of his thoughts and looked at Martin, slightly surprised by the question. He thought for a moment before he said, 'I've never told this story to anyone before... Can you keep a secret?' He hesitated as if ready to change his mind and then said, 'Ah, it was such a long time ago now, I don't suppose anyone will care too much.'

Hector was hooked and he eagerly waited to be landed with the story.

Martin relaxed into his anecdote. 'I can remember the exact moment when I decided to become a dealer in antiquities. It was in 1972. It was like I didn't have a say in the matter – I was *chosen*. I was a student at art college at the time and during the May break I visited Rome to look at some of the best art in the world. And that's why on that particular Whitsunday I was in Saint Peter's Church.' Martin checked Hector's expression to see if that information meant anything to him; the unchanging muscles told him Hector was listening but what he'd heard so far didn't spark any recognition.

'Well, that Whitsun in seventy-two is notorious in art history and I was there. I was in the queue of people filing past the magnificent artworks in the church. The prized sculpture was – and still is – Pietà, by Michelangelo. Today, if you went to see it, it's behind a bullet-proof screen, but then... then you could view it unimpeded.'

A flicker of insight registered on Hector's face. Martin continued with his story.

'I was on my own and swivelling my head like a top to take it all in when I heard a man shout out, "I am Jesus Christ – risen from the dead!" The cry was followed by a sickening crack of something solid being broken, then another crack, then another. I turned my head to look in the direction of this unnatural sound. What I saw was so shocking and surreal that I couldn't take it in at first – and neither could the vast majority of the crowd who, like me, just gawped, frozen to the spot. Standing next to

Michelangelo's masterpiece stood a bearded man with long reddish hair. He held a hammer and he was doing the unthinkable: swinging it with his full might onto the statue. I watched as several more blows rained down on the stone. When the left arm of Mary broke at the elbow and fell to the ground with a sickening clatter of broken marble, it roused some people from their shock. I watched several men jump over the barrier and up the few steps of the altar to fall on the attacker. The first man – an off-duty firefighter, I later learned – grabbed the attacker by the hair and yanked him away from the sculpture, preventing him from hitting it any more. Then all hell broke loose.

'Some people moved to join the men swarming over the attacker, who had disappeared from my view by now, some remained transfixed and yet others started to notice the chips of marble scattered on the floor around their feet. Some old ladies started crossing themselves and calling out to save the pieces as if the chips were the blood of Christ Himself or something. That's when I looked on the floor around me and that's when I noticed a piece of marble near my foot.

'It was a large fragment, mostly smooth. I then recognized it as a nose. Without thinking, I bent down to pick it up before anyone could stand on it and break it into smaller pieces. Again without thinking, I pocketed the piece for safekeeping as people all around me were now jostling and I needed both my hands to fend them off.

'After five minutes some kind of order was restored. The guards had come by then and hustled the attacker away. Women were weeping at the sight of the desecrated statue, men were furious with the attacker and were talking in loud voices. We were all in shock. Then a rumour started going round that a bomb was in the church. That was it, then – panic ensued and we all headed for the exit, terrified that a bomb was going to go off.

'Outside, I kept moving as far away from the church as fast as the crowds would let me. The entire plaza was a heaving mass of old women, anxious parents, screaming kids and confused tourists.

'Eventually, the crowds thinned out and I felt safe from any kind of explosion near the church. I stood on a street corner for ages trying to calm down, thinking about what had just happened.'

There was a long pause as Martin relived the moment. Hector gently urged him on with his story: 'But you still had the nose?'

Martin quickly came round from his distraction. 'Yeah, I suddenly remembered the marble piece in my pocket. I was going to pull it out to take a look at it right there in the street but then I realized that might be unwise so I stopped and pretended to look for something in another pocket.

'I went into a café and ordered a coffee to think about things. My heart was racing – one of the most famous works of art in the world had just been vandalized and I had a piece of it – how lucky was that?

'I went to the toilet and into one of the cubicles to get a better look at the piece of marble. I remember looking up along the edge of the cubicle to check if anyone was peering over before producing the marble – I was that nervous.' He laughed at the thought.

'I looked at it closely. The nose was in perfect condition except where it had broken off and then it was jagged and sharp. That's when I thought about the hand of Michelangelo touching this very piece of marble that I was holding, smoothing it beautifully with immense skill and devotion.

'And that's what started my interest in antiques.'

Hector gave an incredulous laugh. 'Wow! That's an amazing story, but what happened to the nose?'

'Well, no one knew I had it and I didn't want to go back to the church that day to return it because of the bomb scare so I went back to my hotel to get my case and watch the news. I was flying out that evening so I didn't have much time to think about it too much.

'When I got home I followed all the reports of the attack. They'd collected all the fragments of marble they could find and were going to fit them together like a fiendishly complex jigsaw puzzle and then glue them. I think it was in the back of my mind to post the nose to the church but then I thought what if it got lost? I suppose I could have written to tell them I had it and did they want to come and collect it but I suspect at the back of my mind I was probably thinking of keeping it. As time went by I got more attached to the piece and the restorers were talking about using a piece of marble cut out of Mary's back to create a new nose and I figured, what the hell, the masterpiece was going to be okay, so I stopped feeling guilty and kept the nose.'

Hector's mouth was open as if he were gasping for air. 'So you... you still have the nose?'

Martin looked intently into the eyes of Hector as he answered with a mischievous look: 'Yes.' He paused deliberately before he added, 'Do you want to see it?'

Hector cackled hysterically. 'Do I want to see it!? Do bears shit in the woods? Wait, is it here – in the yard?'

Martin nodded. He put down his glass and went to the big safe in his office and unlocked it with a key. From the safe he got another bunch of keys.

'Wait here,' he said.

A couple of minutes later Martin returned holding a small vitrine. He carefully handed it to Hector.

Hector slowly raised the vitrine to his face with as much tenderness as he might have used with one of the breasts of his first true love. Inside the glass dome, nestled on a red velvet cushion, was a piece of marble shaped elegantly into a nose.

'Touched by the hand of Michelangelo,' Hector murmured.

Martin waited. Then Hector said, 'Would you ever consider selling it?'

Martin pretended to be surprised by this question and gave the impression of thinking seriously. And he was thinking.

He was thinking, *I love this game*.

The Cult of Motivation

Grapes? Should she have brought grapes? That's the traditional thing to bring when visiting a hospital. Jane stopped by the shop in the hospital reception area and looked at the products on offer. Most of it was trash – sweets and greetings cards. She wondered why sweets were even allowed in hospitals; sugar is nearly as bad as tobacco in terms of harm, and tobacco isn't sold on hospital premises. She felt uncomfortable with so many slow-moving people milling close by her, she kept expecting one of them to bumble into her and impede her progress. She liked to have space around her. Sometimes she put herself in spaces so isolated that the nearest person was hundreds of miles away. That was bliss.

She wondered if hospitals ever felt deserted. Every time she'd been in one it was always busy. Maybe that was because it was invariably at A&E. Perhaps if she'd been on a recovery ward, say, during a Tuesday morning in August, a hospital might have seemed quiet.

She settled on a paperback book from the shop - *Gone Girl* by Gillian Flynn. It was a thriller novel and not the kind of book that she would typically buy. She almost exclusively bought business-related books. Even though the person she was visiting was in the same industry as her and would appreciate a self-help business book, she decided that something less taxing on the mind was more appropriate. And, she reasoned, a book would keep his boredom at bay for a lot longer than a bunch of grapes.

Striding down a corridor in her flat shoes and at a speed that made her shoulder-length blond hair wave gracefully, she passed several unattended trolleys with inert patients lying on them that reminded her of fully laden shopping trolleys left abandoned in the area beyond the checkout zone. She was sure she could detect a faint whiff of despair hanging over them. Engaging in extreme pursuits, as she did, attuned her to that type of thing.

She was heading for ward 42 on Gate 11. At least the signage in the hospital was organized and easy to follow even if the choice of 'gate' as a signifier was a little odd for a hospital. The word automatically suggested 'departures' to her but now that she thought about it, it could also mean 'arrivals', which would be appropriate for a maternity wing.

As a professional speaker she had trained herself to evaluate any kind of formalized communication system that she happened to come across in case she could use it as an example of good or bad practice during one of her speeches. The hospital signage was so far ticking the 'excellent' box.

Her enquiries had told her that John had a private room within the NHS hospital. Secretly she approved of this: John was a successful speaker and it was befitting of his status that he have such privileges.

Outside the door to his room Jane stopped to look at her Breitling watch. She calculated she had twenty minutes maximum before she had to leave the room to get to her next meeting so she set the vibrating alarm to go off after this time. She knocked on the door and listened with a highly tuned ear. A mumbled groan came through the wood and she interpreted this as consent to enter.

John was sat up in bed holding a digital tablet with his one good arm. His right arm – or what was left of it – was heavily bandaged. He looked up slowly and squinted through glazed eyes. Gradually he made out the shape of

Jane, as lithe as a leopard in her close-fitting white top and tight blue jeans.

'Jane! This is a swurprise,' mumbled John, still coming round from the anaesthetic and looking a lot older than his thirty-six years.

Jane ghosted silently to his side and planted a kiss on his cheek.

'I've brought you a book,' she said as she placed it on his bedside cabinet. 'It's a thriller – to stay in keeping with your misadventure.' She made sure she had proper eye contact with him before she continued: 'I came as soon as I could. I couldn't believe it when I heard the news. I'm so sorry, John.'

John's eyes moistened. 'Thank you, Jane, it means so much to me that you've paid a visit – and so soon! I hope it hasn't inconvenienced you much. I know how busy your schedule is.'

'As luck would have it, I've got a speaking engagement here in the city this evening so fate made it almost certain that I would be visiting you today. How are you feeling now?' Jane asked this as she turned the plastic chair by the side of the bed ninety degrees to face him better when she sat down.

'Comfwutably numb,' John said with a smile. 'I can't feel much... the drugs are still having an effect.'

Jane took the tablet from his left hand and placed it on the bed before slipping her own hand into his. She squeezed tight. 'I'm so sorry this terrible accident has happened to you. It must be devastating. Of all the things to befall—' It was her intention to say 'a motivational speaker' but then in the circumstances she thought it inappropriate and finished unconvincingly with 'a man so young'.

'Do you want to talk about it or would you prefer to chat about unimportant things?'

'You know me, Jane, my professional brand is one of uncompromising honesty. I don't hide from the truth. As a motivational speaker I always call a spade a spade and a chainsaw a chainsaw.'

'Well, at least you'll have something hugely personal to talk about when you're next on stage.' As soon as she'd uttered the words, Jane was regretting them. In the context – so soon after the accident – they seemed flippant, but then John said something that immediately made her worries inconsequential.

'Yes, that's the whole point.'

'What is?' Jane asked. 'I don't understand. What's the whole point?'

'Cutting my arm off.'

In her years of facing many unexpected crises during her arduous expeditions she had become accustomed to thinking on her feet and instantly assessing a dire situation in a calm and rational manner but this one sentence had taken her completely by surprise. She went through the list of possible reactions with which to respond and decided on the one where she laughed and said, 'I'm glad to see you haven't lost your sense of humour, John. Keep positive, that's the spirit.'

'I wasn't joking.'

Jane studied his expression in the same way she might study a blade-thin snow ridge for signs of treachery before attempting to negotiate it.

'John, you've had a terrible accident. You lost your arm after injuring yourself with a chainsaw. What are you trying to tell me?'

'It wasn't an accident.'

Jane remained silent, her eyes burning into his. John felt compelled to continue.

'I did it to myself. It was an active decision I'd made.'

Jane fought the urge to slap his face as she might have done to a colleague who had begun to talk deliriously during one of her expeditions. 'John, you're not making any sense. You seem to be telling me that you deliberately... cut your arm off.'

'That's right, I took control of my life. I made a choice to change something that was holding me back.'

Jane was still in denial. She said, 'I think you might be hallucinating, John. Perhaps you're tired or still under the influence of the anaesthetic. Rational people don't go around injuring a perfectly healthy arm on purpose.'

John's eyes suddenly filled with passion. 'I had an epiphany, Jane. The logic was sound. I've never been more certain in my life, and you know what we say – "Face your fears and get out of your comfort zone".'

Jane studied the man she thought she had known for the past six years. He was one of the most conscientious speakers she'd ever met; always did his homework, always delivered the passion on stage. But she hadn't expected a stunt like this.

'Why did you do it, John?'

'Because I'm committed to the cause of speaking. I want to be the best in the world at what I do, so like any top athlete I undergo whatever training I think will improve my performance. I realized that my life story lacked any real pain, it was too... privileged, I guess. So then it hit me. Create a real obstacle, a physical one with no chance of turning back. I mean, in a way, that's what you do every time you go on an expedition.'

'That's different and you know it. I assess all the risks beforehand and I take precautions to avoid any danger.'

'The best precaution is to not go in the first place. That produces zero risk.'

'Don't be so naive, there's no such thing as zero risk. Every time you climb into a car you're taking a huge risk. But that doesn't mean you should be reckless in your driving and look for danger. Life is only beautiful because we know it's temporary.'

'Exactly! And losing an arm proves that – don't you see? In our profession we're the thought leaders, we lead by example. I have to push myself the hardest otherwise I wouldn't be authentic when I'm on stage and I ask people to overcome their own obstacles.'

'John, you're already a successful motivational speaker. Why would you do this to yourself?'

'My plan is to learn to play the piano as well as fly an aeroplane – with just one arm. If I can't live by my own philosophy what's the point of promoting it? I'd just be a hypocrite. You know, I always felt a little cheated that I had a normal upbringing. My parents helped me to find my first job through their contacts and I never really had to struggle with anything in life, whereas some motivational speakers had the perfect background to form resilience and perseverance – poverty, abuse, drug addiction, disability. Such material! They had a head start on everyone else.'

Jane's expression was inscrutable. She was thinking hard. Then her face became animated as she decided on a plan.

'Who have you told about this decision to cut off your arm?' she asked.

'No one, just you, you're the first,' he said in a congratulatory tone.

'And I'm going to be the last, John. Do you hear me?'

'What difference does it make who knows?'

Despite herself, Jane rolled her eyes. 'Think about it; if this gets out you become known as the motivational speaker who cut a perfectly healthy limb off his own body to prove a point. Everything might make perfect sense to you but as we know, that's irrelevant when it comes to the bigger picture – it doesn't matter what happened in history, it's what people *believe* happened that's important.

'You've currently got a successful career going as a motivational speaker. If I were a client looking to book a speaker and I heard your story I would consider it too troubling for my audience. It's not the lost limb that's the problem, it's your choosing to do it that is. The corporate world is hugely conservative, as you well know.

'You want to be the best, right?' Jane held his eyes and waited for a definite answer. John nodded slowly. 'Say it.' Jane persisted.

'Yes, I want to be the best.'

'Good. Well this is how to achieve it. You've lost an arm. You were a successful speaker when you lost it but that didn't stop you from carrying on with your career; in fact it spurred you on to be even more passionate and motivated to succeed, got it?'

John nodded again. 'Got it,' he said.

'But you lost your arm in an accident. In. An. Accident. Do you understand me?'

John nodded. He was starting to see the logic.

When Jane saw his comprehension she put real feeling into her closing argument. 'You just need to show people how you overcame that setback, that's all. You can still be the best in your profession. If you try to explain to the audience your motive you will be confusing them – *the explanation does not add value to your message, it reduces it.*

'And here's the thing: once you've recovered and demonstrated your ability to overcome this recent obstacle you'll be able to double your fees because you're already a successful speaker so the impact of your message is twice as powerful – you proved the truth of what you speak! And think of the book sales, John, the invitations to conferences, TEDx talks...'

This was language John understood. 'Of course! You're absolutely right. Nothing changes in practical terms whether I tell anyone or not, does it? I've still got my challenges after losing my arm. Yes! Yes! Good thinking. It was an unfortunate accident.'

Jane breathed a heavy sigh. She'd made a convincing argument. 'Good. And don't put any more limbs in a combine-harvester or whatever, to improve your career any further, okay?'

'I won't, I promise.'

Jane got up from her chair and hugged him gently, mindful of his surgery. She kissed him on the cheek.

'I have to go. A potential client wants to chat over coffee.'

'A big prospect?'

'A multinational. Keynote and consultancy.'

'Nice. Hope it goes well.'

'Thanks, John. Take care. I'll call you tomorrow and make sure you remember our agreement.' Jane made it clear there was no room for negotiation on this point.

'Thanks for visiting. You've probably saved my life.'

'And it wouldn't be the first time,' smiled Jane as the watch on her wrist started vibrating. She left the room and once outside stopped the watch alarm.

As she walked down the corridor she felt a high similar to the one she usually experienced when walking off a stage after 'killing' the audience. She had just given one of the finest performances of her career but now her mind was racing with possibilities and she didn't have the time to glory in her prowess as a speaker.

Driving along the motorway, Jane allowed her mind to wander over the conversation she's just had. She was in the outside lane travelling at 85 mph when she came up behind a blue BMW dawdling along at 75 mph. She checked the middle lane and saw it was clear of traffic. She flashed the BMW but it made no attempt to get out of her way. Without a moment's hesitation Jane pulled into the middle lane and gunned the accelerator to blaze past the BMW. She threw a quick glance at the car as she passed. Her confirmation bias was confirmed: it was a white-shirted, white, male driver giving her a filthy look. He sounded his horn as she undertook him.

She returned to her train of thought.

Able-bodied, she was an expert skier but nowhere near the standard of Olympic athletes. She knew this because she was once briefly in a training squad that included a medal hopeful. No one in the squad could keep pace with her. If she had tried to be an Olympic competitor herself she would have been an also-ran and thus a nobody.

In the Paralympics however...

She imagined what a gold medal would do for her speaking career. She could probably triple her current fees and still be able to enjoy the physical pursuits she was so passionate about – a win-win.

She was attractive too – perhaps a media career could be had once her competitive days were coming to an end. Her foot unconsciously pressed on the accelerator as her imagination raced ahead...

Someone had to be the first to trail-blaze a new idea. After all, didn't motivational speakers regularly remind their audiences that ideas established today were initially considered heretical when first proposed? If she had documentary evidence on video, she could then claim to be the pioneer of this new trend when the time was right to announce it. Because new challenges were becoming harder to find in a world with fewer and fewer risks, people had to find unusual ways to create epic adventures. She would go down in history as being the first speaker to fashion her own challenges in a unique way.

Jane was becoming more enamoured with the idea, adrenalin flowed in her veins and she felt good to be alive.

Now, which foot should she lose – the left or the right?

Lazarus Corps

The ten thousand strong audience had been waiting for nearly an hour for the show to start. Most of them were absorbed with their phones, staring vacantly at the glowing screens that threw eerie light onto their faces.

Rancid, the PR intern from the production company organizing the show, was standing near the stage and looking at his own phone, monitoring the social media comments about #malariadeathring. Most of the audience were clearly becoming pissed off at the delay but were trying to be amusing about it in their comments.

The delay was being carefully stage-managed. With high overheads and penalty clauses in the contract about time overruns at the venue, the entire show was designed to run like clockwork. It was Rancid's job to gauge whether the 'rebellious' attitude of the tardy band was returning any dividends. A debrief after the show would discuss the efficacy of the tactic and decide whether to continue the practice or not at future events.

Rancid checked the time on his phone – show time!

A swelling bass tone in the background grew louder until it reached the maximum decibel rating the concert hall was allowed to have by law. It reverberated in Rancid's chest. He looked up from his phone at the vast stage, empty of people but festooned with equipment poking through the shallow layer of dry ice like skyscrapers piercing cloud cover. A column of light, like a biblical portent, was falling onto the stage. The audience, as one, raised their phones into the air to video the moment.

From the side of the stage emerged a lone figure walking towards the spotlight. It was a young man with voluminous dark hair tumbling over his shoulders. He was wearing a loose-fitting white poet shirt tucked into brown leather trousers that were accessorized with an ornate buckle belt – the aficionados in the audience immediately recognized it as *the* silver Zuni Navajo Concho belt made famous by its wearer.

The figure reached the shaft of light drilling into the stage. He stepped into the beam and the bass note subsided. Jim Morrison stared at the audience. He stood silently for a few seconds, allowing the audience to take in the extraordinary detail of his clothes, his hair, his belt... A huge screen above the stage relayed the live moment. Then he spoke to the crowd in a husky drawl: 'Ladies and gentlemen... Malaria Death Ring.' He then turned and walked off the stage the same way he had come.

To the cheers of the audience, the members of Malaria Death Ring emerged from the centre of the stage on a hydraulic riser. They were face-painted and costumed so exotically that they made Captain Beefheart and his Magic Band from the acid days of the '60s look like a team of bank clerks on their first day at work. A distinctive intro chord from one of their hits was struck on a guitar and the show kicked off.

*

Months before the show, the production team had their regular meeting at the record company headquarters. They sat around the glass boardroom table.

'Siobhan, who do we have introducing the band on the fifth?'

Martin asked this question while scrolling through his digital tablet. Siobhan was on the other side of the table flicking her dyed hair away from her face. The others at the table looked at her.

'We've currently got the President of the United States as the introducer.'

'Which one?' Martin asked.

'Donald Trump,' answered Siobhan.

Hugh, a young, handsome man sitting next to Siobhan, said, 'Isn't he getting a bit... clichéd? I mean, how often can he say "this is the best band, you're going to see, the best show ever" before it gets too predictable? Besides, I'm reliably informed that Donald Trump is going to be introducing Horse Blood on the same night in Birmingham. Surely, we want to be a bit more exclusive than that.' He looked at Martin for support. Martin continued to peer at his tablet.

'Who told you that?' asked Martin still looking at his tablet.

'Peter Pinkjacket,' said Hugh.

'Pinkjacket! He's a coke-head; you can't trust anything he says,' yelled Siobhan.

Martin looked up from his tablet, sensing a time-wasting spat between his team members. He addressed the five people sitting at the table. 'Reliable or not, I think it's worth looking at other options anyway. This is a big gig for Death Ring as it coincides with the album launch, so it might be worth exploring something... unusual. Andy, do you know of anything being developed that we might be able to use?'

Andy was the geek with his finger on the digital pulse of innovation.

'I hear Jim Morrison is going to be available soon,' he said.

'Whooa! He would be cool!' said Mike, the creative executive who knew his rock history.

'Really? Any idea how much he would be?' asked Martin.

'It wouldn't be that much more than Donald Trump, but there would obviously be a premium for exclusivity. The downside is, the quality wouldn't be quite as good as

Trump, as the archive footage is so poor. Comparatively,' Andy added.

Mike said, 'But it's been so long since anyone saw him in the flesh it wouldn't matter. To the people in the audience he would be real enough. And, as we own The Doors' back catalogue, it could generate sales from curious onlookers who haven't heard of him.'

'I'm liking the idea of Jim Morrison more than Donald Trump,' said Martin as he glanced at Siobhan. 'Morrison has more... gravitas than Trump, and Mike is right, we need to consider the trade-off between the extra cost of the avatar and the possible revenue from fresh sales. See if you can fix that up, would you?'

Siobhan made a note on her phone.

Later, at around midnight, Siobhan made a video call to Leee from Lazarus Corporation.

'It looks like we're going to run with Jim Morrison, Leee, do you know if the avatar will be ready for the fifth? We just need him to say "Ladies and gentlemen, Malaria Death Ring".'

Leee was suitably rock and roll, with a shaven head and dark glasses. He responded from his sunlit office in LA, 'Yep, he's just about ready for a trial run and he looks be-oootiful. We've rendered him in his prime at twenty-two. You'll be the first to have him.'

Yeah, *after some American outfit*, thought Siobhan.

'Fabulous,' said Siobhan. 'Consider this confirmation. I'll send the official request through in about fifteen minutes.'

*

In the old days, living celebrities would open a show for a band in person but this entailed so many problems for the production team – with egos, riders, and reliability issues – that an exasperated executive came up with a novel idea.

He got the idea from a development first seen at conferences. A speaker, who was many thousands of miles away, would be projected onto a stage during a live event. To the audience it looked pretty much as if this speaker was in the room, not in a studio on the other side of the world. They could even conduct a Q&A session with them afterwards and still maintain the illusion of reality.

It was only a small step to imagine a pre-recorded message given by a celebrity being projected onto a stage, but this still involved getting the cooperation of the celebrity in the first place.

Then some digital artists armed with fast computers and lots of start-up funding took it one step further. They had seen the online videos that mocked certain politicians with mashed-up broadcast footage of their old speeches. Fast and clever editing made the politician say or sing outrageous things that the public understood to be nearer to the truth of things.

What these digital artists did was to create a believable hologram of a living celebrity purely from footage that was available online. Hugely sophisticated algorithms could extrapolate new scenarios based on the known mannerisms of the subject. A programmer could then feed any body movements and dialogue that they required into the program to generate a convincing representation of the celebrity on a stage at a live event. The result was the current fashion for having a big name introduce an act. The day of an avatar indistinguishable from the real celebrity (at least viewed from a short distance) had arrived.

Real celebrities were a pain in the arse. Avatars were the future.

The celebrities on offer – alive or dead – were growing by the month. However, the older the celebrity, the more expensive they tended to be as the processing power needed to resurrect them was higher due to the paucity of material and the poorer quality of the data.

Having a celebrity introduce an act with the line 'Ladies and gentlemen, please welcome X' was just the right length to make the process commercially viable for medium-sized acts. And once they had been generated, smaller acts could purchase a licence to use the same file but with a slight alteration for whatever name they required the avatar to speak.

Of course, celebrities were outraged at the appropriation of their intellectual property and lawsuits were quickly filed but once the lawyers started to look into the case many loopholes and omissions were revealed. The technology was too new for the old law. The avatar creators argued that they weren't pretending that the actual celebrity was opening the show; they were completely upfront about them being a *deepfake*. The lawyers weren't even sure if the image fell under the legislation designed for artworks or not – it was a lawless frontier.

Such were the uncertainties of these cases that they were quickly thrown out of court and the aggrieved celebrities suddenly realized what it must feel like to be a production worker in a factory and have your job stolen by a tireless robot.

Overnight, celebrities got increasingly shy about appearing on any media that recorded them walking, talking or even cutting a ribbon with a pair of scissors. Lawyers of the celebrities ordered that old media be deleted from video sites and they lobbied the legislators to protect the rights of their unfortunate clients.

By that time, however, the innovators had already banked terabytes of data ready to analyze and render into new compliant ghosts.

It wasn't long before filmmakers started to look at the costs of creating a full-length movie using digitally reproduced actors based on real actors – but these new actors wouldn't throw a tantrum, get coked up in their trailers or even age over time.

Some gossip columnists enjoyed the schadenfreude of celebrities losing status and earnings because of the avatars. Writers felt especially smug; they enjoyed renewed status as the spoken lines that the avatars delivered became more important than the celebrities themselves.

That didn't last long, however. 'Deep learning' algorithms became creative and started to churn out copy that humans found amusing, dazzling or moving based on what the audience had previously found amusing, dazzling and moving. The algorithms even learned to apply context and topicality to their output.

Then Bill Hicks got a new show. It was completely written by algorithms. The show even used the name 'Bill Hicks' as the owners of his estate realized it was useless fighting the onslaught of new technology and they might as well take a slice of the pie through licensing agreements rather than go hungry.

The show was a smash. The persona of Bill Hicks lent itself beautifully to some of the surreal imagery that the algorithm conjured up out of its mathematical processes and it even managed to come up with a routine that included some self-referential jokes about artificial intelligence being too clever by five eighths for dumb humans.

All the creativity in the show was machine-generated and the only thing left for humans to do was to consume it.

Had he been alive, Bill Hicks would have—well, the algorithm will determine that for us.

Four Religious Leaders

The four bearded men sat around a table. Each was dressed in a different coloured robe.

'Gentlemen,' said the man dressed in a saffron robe, 'I've come up with an idea. We all realize we're going to die at some point, agreed?' The other men looked suspiciously at Saffron Robe but they all nodded their heads. 'But, I've figured out that afterwards we continue to live. I've done this by studying trees that die and then watching fungus emerge from them. We probably do the same. Except we're not fungus in this afterlife I've seen. No, my idea is this: we are born into another world and live a similar life there.'

The other men looked impressed.

'And not only that,' Saffron Robe continued, 'but you get to live in this next world for... three hundred years.'

The other men thought about this before the man in the blue robe said, 'Well, I'd pretty much worked this out for myself too but in my revelations it was shown to me that when we're born into the next world, we come back as grown men. No need for all that baby nonsense, and we get to live for... a *thousand* years.'

The men reflected deeply on this information until a voice broke the silence.

'Purgatory.'

This came from the black-robed man. 'You've missed out an important element to the afterlife that I've spotted. I've discovered there is a secret cave in the next world where people wait around trying to work out how to reach the new world. This is where obnoxious people have to wait for, oh, two thousand years before they—'

Before he could finish he was interrupted by the fourth man, dressed in a white robe: 'Yes, I too have discovered an afterlife. But in this world, you come back as a young man at the height of your sexual powers, you can bring your entire family and friends with you to live there AND...' he looked round at everyone to make sure his point was fully understood, 'they get to live in this luxury *for ever.*'

'For ever?' the other men chorused.

'Yep,' and White Robe banged his fist on the table to emphasize his point, 'in my afterlife, no one dies again. Ever.'

The other men could see they'd all been bested.

After a brief silence, Black Robe said, 'Won't that get a bit boring?'

White Robe came back instantly: 'You can't get bored. It's not called "heaven" for nothing.'

The three other men fiddled with their beards for a minute before Blue Robe said, 'Well, I've just remembered, in my world, when you enter it as a virile young man, you're given twenty-four virgins to do what you want with them.'

White Robe raised his white eyebrows at this revelation.

'Who are these virgins?' asked Black Robe.

Blue Robe played for time: 'What do you mean?' he asked.

'Well, they must be the daughters of someone,' persisted Black Robe. 'Is this someone important? I mean, if my daughter was in heaven with me, could she end up being one of *your* virgins?'

Blue Robe looked worried. 'Er, no, they're virgins that haven't lived on earth yet.'

'So these virgins won't know anything about life in this world? Especially about sex?' mused White Robe.

Suddenly, in an angry voice, Black Robe asked, 'Who makes these virgins anyway?'

Blue Robe thinks hard: 'A... man.'

Black Robe pressed home his attack: 'A man in heaven? But if I'm the first guest in heaven, where are my virgins? It's not much of a heaven if I have to start constructing twenty-four virgins as soon as I arrive – and I mean, what I know about female genitalia isn't nearly enough to start stitching one together. And what if I don't want to do anything but laze around?'

Blue Robe felt he was being singled out for his extravagant visions. Gamely, he tried to defend them. 'No, the man, the... er... *Creator* is already there – he's always been there.'

The other men look unconvinced.

Undaunted, Blue Robe revealed his winning hand. 'He's the person responsible for making everything.' Then, as if he were reaching for a pot of money in the centre of the table, he announced emphatically, 'Even this world we're living in now.'

Black Robe leaned across the table and looked Blue Robe in the eye. 'Right... Let me see if I've got this straight. A Creator man makes everything that exists, divides it all up into the temporary and the eternal, we all eventually end up in the eternal where we come back as young men with exactly the same personalities that we had on earth...'

'But I know someone who's a dick,' interrupted Saffron Robe looking pointedly at Blue Robe. 'I wouldn't want him in the same place as me, especially not for eternity. And what about my dog – will he be allowed into this heaven of yours, eh?'

Blue Robe had staked out his territory and he felt he had to defend it, come what may. 'Well, as it happens, I'm not too keen on you either – or your version of heaven, so I'm not going to allow any of your Saffron followers into my heaven. Or your sodding dog!'

Saffron Robe snarled back, 'Oh yeah? Well, I'm going to instruct all my followers to kill on sight any of your followers when they come across them!'

'Right! That's it!'

All the men overturned the table and stood up ready to fight each other. Just then, a booming female voice seemed to fill every molecule of the room. The men were transfixed by its power.

'Gentlemen,' the voice said, 'you have reached the conclusion of my experiment. Thank you. Now, for no logical reason whatsoever, I am going to reset the experiment from the beginning again and run it to see if there are any changes to the results.

'Oh, and I'll keep doing this for all eternity because – well, it just amuses me.'

A Tub of Excrement

The queue for the council waste-recycling centre snakes out of the entrance gates and protrudes onto the adjoining main road and its two-lanes of traffic. I'm waiting at the junction to turn right into the centre behind several other cars but as the filter light turns green no cars in my queue begin to move. The sensible driver at the front of the queue knows he has to wait for a space to avoid causing total gridlock at the junction.

This queue is hardly surprising; it's the first glorious weekend in April and on a sunny Sunday people discover they have tons of rubbish to get rid of so they organize a trip to the tip.

It takes me ten minutes to get across the junction and then a further twenty minutes to crawl my way along the corralled line of traffic to reach the berth of rubbish skips. An attendant is hovering nearby. My window is already down as the weather is so clement.

'Excuse me.' I say to him, 'where do I dispose of toxic waste?'

He's sporting bare arms through his hi-viz vest and the white hard-hat he's wearing is covered in a thin film of dust and grime. It's difficult to tell if this film is new or ancient. He looks at me like a member of the public might view a mad scientist.

'What is it?' he asks uncertainly.

'Sewage,' I reply. There is then what is referred to in theatrical scripts as a *beat* – a pregnant pause full of possibilities. He continues to stare at me with growing suspicion as I sit in my idling car. I feel compelled to volunteer more information. 'It's in a tub.'

Thoughtfully, he considers some options, a couple of which appear unsavoury judging by the fleeting expressions on his face. 'Bin number five,' he offers finally then turns away as if to escape my presence. He hesitates, hurriedly turns back towards me and says with authority, 'Leave it in the tub.'

I acknowledge this instruction with a silent nod and the conga line of traffic forces me to move forward.

I'm mildly amused by this exchange. It was the *'leave it in the tub'* remark that got my imagination mushrooming with ideas, as if the sewage had indeed acted like a fertilizer. What does he think I'm going to do? Stand at the safety barrier above the three-metre-tall skip and pour it into the skip like a bucket of dirty water? And then what? Take the tub home, stowing it in my car boot all smeared with stinking faeces and with little brown tributaries of effluent running down its sides to soak into the black pile of my boot interior? Why did he think I might want to hang onto the tub?

On reflection, I decide that, armed with the information I'd just given him, he was probably being more than reasonable in his remark towards me, although I suppose with me being out of sight he might very well be on his walkie-talkie right this minute speaking in an agitated tone to his supervisor and alerting him or her to my presence. 'We've got a rogue one coming through – sewage mentioned…'

Is sewage toxic, I wonder? And how often does the council waste-recycling centre get it brought to them? Not often, I surmise. Most people have toilets to get rid of such waste.

The more I think about it, the more bizarre my question must have seemed to the attendant. What the hell am I doing driving around with sewage in my car?

Of course it all seems perfectly reasonable to me, being at the epicentre of all the circumstances that led me to this point in time. Each incident was a natural progression from the last incident, as if the sequence were merely describing a parabolic arc of physical inevitability, as you would expect when a ball is thrown into the air and gravity acts upon it.

No, I find it perfectly reasonable to have a five-litre tub of human excrement in my car. For anyone else, though, it must seem slightly strange, even if they were to know I am an artist.

Not that my art involves any outlandish materials. I'm not a conceptual artist like Pierro Manzoni, producing ninety cans of artist's shit, I'm just a run-of-the-mill representational painter using traditional watercolours and oil paints. But even if I were an eccentric performance artist, I would hardly be doing a performance piece at the council waste-recycling centre without any kind of invited audience. No cameras are in tow to document my interactions with the staff at the centre and I don't have any kind of recording device to capture the moment when the human shit (some of which, I admit, is mine) is thrown into bin number five from a height of about three metres. This is definitely no artistic happening.

I've had the tub of excrement for some time now, over two months at least. It has lived at the side of my house in that period, hidden from my neighbours (although it's impossible to tell what's inside the tub just from looking at it – for all they knew, had they came across it, it was still housing premium white emulsion paint – its original contents, as the label on the tub proudly attests).

At that time I still hadn't decided what to do with it but it was still winter so I didn't worry too much about the urgency.

After it had festered for such a length of time outside my house, I was now reluctant to look inside the tub – and why would I want to? Well, if I'm honest, I would like to check a hypothesis, because as I lifted the tub to take to my car I'm sure it felt considerably lighter than when I first filled it with effluent. True, I am relying on my memory, which science has proven to be unreliable, but that didn't stop me imagining an explanation for the weight loss, and I came up with possible bacterial action as an answer. I immediately discounted this hypothesis however as the tub has been sealed with a plastic lid the whole time. I know enough about biology to realize that whatever bacteria have found their way into the excrement, they need oxygen to perform their action. The pathologist part of my brain however is nagging me to take a look and confirm or deny the theory – purely for scientific reasons. I continue to resist the urge.

When I arrive at bin number five, I find the gangway to it roped off and guarded by another bare-armed attendant in high-viz jacket and white hard-hat. I guess some essential procedure needs to be completed before I can dispose of the tub; a quick glance suggests the skip is being removed and emptied.

As I have waited so long in the heated queue of cars to get to this point I am annoyed at this hiatus. The tub swings gently at my side as my heavily gloved hand grips its thin wire handle (made more comfortable by the addition of a rotating plastic cylinder). The attendant notices my annoyance and tries to reassure me with, 'It'll only take a few minutes.'

I give him a thin smile. He then looks down at my load. 'Is that all you've got?' I nod. 'If you want to leave it here, I'll get rid of it for you. It needs to go to the paint skip anyway.'

'Oh great, thanks! But it's not paint…'

The attendant, a man in his late fifties or early sixties with a lived-in face, looks at me expectantly.

'It's … full of excrement.'

The man laughs loudly 'Blimey! I don't think I've ever come across that being thrown away here. Why do you have sewage to throw away – don't you have a toilet?'

For some reason his candour annoys me and without checking my thoughts I blurt out at him, 'Of course I have. Actually I've got three.'

Unmoved, he continues to search my face for an explanation. His trusting eyes, dog-like in their innocence, disarm me.

'What happened was this. I had a blocked drain and when I lifted the man-hole cover on the sewage inspection chamber I discovered a mountain of shit mixed in with those wet-wipes that don't disintegrate in water. The whole thing looked like a tub of meat with veins of white fat running through it.

'I've got some drain rods so I started to poke about trying to clear the blockage but I could see these wet-wipes were tying together and forming a knot. I realized then that it would be a mistake just trying to force them down the pipe so I had the idea of lifting them out with the claw attachment on the drain rod. Of course I couldn't just dump it on the garden so I got an empty paint tub from the garage and filled that with most of the tangled wet wipes along with a load of shit stuck to them.'

He looked at me with a newfound respect. 'Sensible,' he said. 'I'd have done the same. Nothing worse than a blocked sewer pipe. These wet-wipes are a curse on the planet.'

I replied, 'I've banned them from the toilet now. I've told the family they can only use toilet paper.'

'Good,' he said. 'I never use them. It's odd that the government doesn't ban them outright considering all the damage they do to the sewage system. Okay, leave it with me and I'll drop it into the skip.'

'Thanks,' I say as I pass the tub of excrement to his outstretched gloved hand.

I return to my car and in the bright spring sunshine drive out of the compound and back into the flow of one of the pulsing arteries of the Wakefield road system, a system that is threatening to clog up. In my rear-view mirror I see the worsening queue waiting to get into the tip. *They're like the wet-wipes*, I think. *Wet-wipes covered in shit.*

Skin in the Game

The most seemingly insignificant of details can precipitate an entire movement in art. When, in approximately 500 BC, Euthymedes was illustrating a vase with an image of a young warrior, instead of drawing him with both feet viewed from the side aspect as was the custom, he decided to draw one of the feet as viewed from the front and in so doing, accidentally 'invented' foreshortening. The response from his fellow artists was explosive. A door into a new world had been opened for them and they were now free to explore all the possibilities of perspective and dynamic movement. Art never looked back and the world never looked the same again.

And this is why today we remember the name of Jean-Michel Baton. What he did to the art world in his own lifetime was as revolutionary as the invention of abstract art or ready-mades. But I get ahead of myself in this tale. Let's start at the beginning.

Jean-Michel Baton was the youngest of three children born to Cecile and Bertram Baton, who lived in San Francisco. Bertram ran a little tattoo parlour in the Haight-Ashbury district and he was well respected as an artist in the inking circles of the city. It had been Bertram's ambition to be a revolutionary graffiti artist as well-known and respected as Keith Haring but one too many police arrests worked against him and he had to settle for inking skin instead of property.

From a very early age Jean-Michel expressed an interest in drawing and making things. All his toys quickly became marking implements or tools to make things or take them apart. His fascination with the tattoo parlour, and the technology used in it, was unquenchable and he would spend as much time as possible there. When the time came for him to eat or have a nap and one of his parents attempted to remove him from the parlour he would wail incessantly in protest. Eventually a playpen was set up in the cramped area and Jean-Michel would spend hours gazing through the bars watching his father work on a client's skin.

When school attendance was required it was an irritating intrusion into his life but it did have one benefit – it opened his eyes to the possibilities of science and he started to take an interest in the chemistry of the inks his father used.

At the weekends he would often sit in the parlour and sketch the portraits of the customers who were being worked upon. Having this precocious child sat in a corner concentrating so intently on a drawing would amuse the customers no end. Often they would say to him, 'If this picture is any good, son, I'll give you a dollar for it.'

Bertram would smile to himself at their ignorance of his son's abilities for when the time came for Jean-Michel to show them his drawings they would receive a shock: the skill involved in capturing their likenesses belonged to someone with many more years' experience than his tender years could contain. The customer would usually end up buying the portrait for a sum that went far beyond friendly indulgence. 'Hey, Bertie,' a typical customer would say, 'this kid of yours is a better artist than you!'

'And don't I know it. You'd better hang onto that drawing coz one day my boy is gonna be famous – real famous.'

Bertram encouraged his son at every opportunity and guided his development in an attempt to offer him the opportunities he lacked until one day Jean-Michel showed his father a design he'd devised for a tattoo. It was a remarkable design but Bertram had to tell him it wouldn't work in the skin as the colours were too intense and didn't exist for the inks he could buy. Undeterred, Jean-Michel reworked the design using modified colours and his father declared it worthy of a place on the sample wall in the parlour.

Bertram was a canny businessman and he deliberately promoted his son's work above his own, telling his customers how young his son was and what a glittering future he had ahead of him. At first, when customers chose his son's designs, he did the needlework himself but eventually a customer said to him, 'If the design isn't yours, who did the line work?'

'My son. He designed it and laid it out.'

'If he's got such a steady hand, why doesn't he do the inking as well?'

'He's very young so he's at school during the day.'

'Still at school? Jeez. You know what, I don't care. I love this design and I want the artist to do the inking. Is he able to do it at the weekends?'

And so it was that Jean-Michel got to ink his first customer. He was barely thirteen years old.

Bertram had no qualms about letting his son ink the customer: he'd seen the practice sessions on countless grapefruits that Jean had completed.

Over the years, Jean-Michel's developing skill as an artist amazed everyone and his fame began to spread. There was a cachet about showing your tattoo and saying it was a Biscuit original (the nickname given to Jean-Michel) and the business had to move to bigger premises in a more upmarket location. But this was not the real genius of Jean-Michel. He was as much a scientist as he was an artist and he studied the chemistry of inks and pigments along with the cell structure of human skin. He was constantly experimenting with different combinations and before long he managed to develop a colour that made the parlour the talk of California. No other parlour could reproduce this colour and wearers of it were immediately identified as owning a Biscuit tattoo. His rise to stardom had begun in earnest.

Bertram spent a large part of his savings in patenting the ink. Soon after that, he retired from the parlour and concentrated solely on promoting and managing his son's burgeoning career.

Then one day, DJ Moran, an up-and-coming star of the football field, contacted Bertram and offered his arm to Jean-Michel to do with whatever he liked – DJ wouldn't interfere in the design at all. Bertram immediately saw the publicity potential in this story and negotiated a mutually beneficial contract with DJ. They presented the story as a sponsorship deal: DJ would advertize the services of Jean-Michel on his arm through the use of the special colour but such was the value of the artwork that he wouldn't be paid anything for doing so. Not only that but DJ had to sign a contract that forbade him from having any more tattoos done anywhere else on his body – unless it was done by Jean. There was no way they could realistically enforce the contract but the novelty of it did its job and the media fed on the news, putting DJ and Jean in the spotlight for several days.

Once the actual work was completed, the media attention returned with a vengeance. The sleeve design was mesmerising and Jean had introduced an additional new colour that he'd specially developed for the raw sienna-coloured skin of DJ.

Jean-Michel had captured the zeitgeist. His talent combined with Bertram's showmanship meant that the art establishment had to take him seriously.

At the age of twenty-one, Jean-Michel was already a famous artist working exclusively in the medium of ink. His consummate skill extended into the chemistry of the pigments and he could achieve effects with the inks that no other tattoo artist could hope to match. The apotheosis of his skill was reached when he manufactured a pigment that shone gold when in the skin. This was that pivotal moment in art history when everything changes. The possibilities for bodily decoration were vast.

Only the richest celebrities could afford his work now and the way they vied for his limited time was reminiscent of the way popes and kings used to compete to commission the work of a favoured artist of the era.

The art world however had trouble with his work. It looked down on his successes – he was *just* a tattoo artist. This infuriated Jean as none of the established art periodicals acknowledged his contribution to art by writing articles about his developments.

One day Bertram sat down and did the math. The waiting list of clients meant that Jean-Michel would be busy for the next two years, at least. The fees were so astronomical that neither he nor Jean-Michel would be short of money again. During a rare evening of quiet, Bertram had a discussion with his son.

'Jean-Michel, I've tried to guide your career as best I can and I have to say that I think I've done a pretty good job doing it. It's nearly all down to your genius, of course, but I can tell you that you've reached a point where you can now do whatever you want and make your mark in the world.'

Jean-Michel smiled at the well-worn pun.

Bertram continued: 'You don't have to accept commissions from rich patrons anymore. I know you're a real artist alongside the likes of Dali and Picasso. If the snobs in the art establishment can't see that it's their fault; history shows they're always behind the curve. You've reached a time in your life when you can concentrate on your art and think about the kind of legacy you're going to leave behind. You should be thinking about creating your "David" or "Last Supper".'

And so it was that they plotted and hatched their scheme.

A few weeks later Bertram announced to the millions of subscribers to the Biscuit livestream that Jean-Michel was looking for a person who would submit their entire skin to him to carry a masterpiece. Jean-Michel would study the form and movements of the chosen man and create a design that capitalized on them in exactly the same way that some of the cave paintings used the natural contours of the rock to suggest the muscle form of the animals being depicted. Every millimetre of the skin, including the top of the head, had to be available to Jean-Michel, the master tattooist.

The response was unprecedented. Tens of thousands of young men submitted photos of their naked bodies. Teams of assistants gradually winnowed these submissions down to a level that was manageable for Jean-Michel to go through the remaining selection and shortlist a handful that would be flown to his studio to be studied intensely by the master.

Eventually, a beautiful young man with flawless, white skin was chosen. Fernando Swartz was going to become a world-famous work of art.

The work took just over a year to complete. Often, Fernando had to be sedated during the many hours that Jean-Michel worked on the skin. The work was taking so long partly because Jean-Michel was developing special pigments to achieve some spectacular results, and partly because the design was so intricate and involved the entire body.

Finally the work was completed and a press conference was arranged. During the conference, only the torso of the dazzling work was revealed as a kind of trailer but everyone could see it was a masterpiece that rivalled anything on the Sistine Chapel ceiling.

Then the second part of the plan came into effect. Fernando was chosen not only for his beautiful body and skin but for his social skills too. As a living work of art, he would be required to exhibit his body to a curious public.

Fernando was invited to attend various high-profile functions just so that guests could view the tattoos close up. This had been the plan all along and Fernando had signed a contract that obliged him to accept these lucrative appearances for the next five years.

Eventually, the guest appearances became performance pieces in themselves and the organizers of the events requested different levels of undress for the occasion. Often times this would mean stripping down to a pair of swimming trunks, after which Fernando would work the room, moving from group to group, allowing them to marvel at the incredible colours and design. The totality of the design, however, extended into his groin, genitals and buttocks, and the patrons started to insist on getting their money's worth by having all the artwork on display. So the requests were for total nudity, regardless of the sensibilities of the people attending the function. Fernando was sometimes placed in a viewing room so the guests could choose to view the masterpiece or not, if they were of delicate sensibilities. The fixed appearance fee covered Jean-Michel's royalty, Fernando's fee and the fee of his minder.

One of the changes in society that was precipitated by these performance events was that Fernando's nudity was viewed as art rather than nudity in much the same way that female nudes in art galleries would be considered acceptable by the visiting public. Over time, large numbers of traditionally conservative Americans who once would have lynched him for contravening the code of propriety were prepared to allow Fernando to wander naked through corridors of power.

Finally, the established art market had to take tattoos seriously. There was too much interest in it for them to ignore it any longer. The creation of a living artwork was perfect fodder for the intellectuals to angst over. Countless articles followed in the most prestigious periodicals. But a strange dilemma overtook the art market: the living artwork was worth a fortune but no one was sure how this fortune could be monetized.

This was another practical joke played on the art market by Jean-Michel and his father. Just like the 'ready-mades' or the tins of artist's shit, they were provoking the art world with ideas that defied containment. For far too long the art of the tattooist had been looked down upon by the art élite but now the élite were fighting over themselves to associate with an artist who only worked in that one medium.

Such was the demand for the designs of Jean-Michel that he completed two more masterpieces in the next five years: another young man calling himself Art Boy and a young woman called The End (as soon as they were chosen as subjects they adopted these stage names to maximize their new-found fame).

Then tragedy struck. At the height of his powers, Jean-Michel died. An aneurism ended his life at the age of thirty-one. The art world was stunned.

Suddenly, tattooing's greatest ever artist was gone and there were only three living artworks of his left in the world. The market went crazy.

Then Fernando died.

His friends said it came as no surprise to them; Fernando was as famous as any rock star and had the lifestyle that went with the fame. Also, he had little talent; he was simply wearing the genius of Jean-Michel like a model on a catwalk. He was the embodiment of the imposter syndrome. There was much speculation about the pressures of being a living piece of artwork in constant demand all over the world. Sure, Fernando had a cut-off point in his contract that restricted the number of gigs he was required to complete in a year, but the seductive celebrity lifestyle has a corrosive addiction that few can resist. The sex and drugs and constant media pressure caught up with him and he took his own life at the age of twenty seven, thereby joining the exclusive club of rock 'n' roll legends who died at that same age. Fernando poisoned himself with a cocktail of drugs. One tabloid newspaper even commented how 'fortunate' it was that he'd chosen poison instead of a more destructive end that could have ruined the artwork for the funeral photos.

*

The pathologist opened the drawer marked 'Fernando Swartz' and slid the drawer out with the cadaver on it for the two men to see. A white sheet covered the body. Standing behind the pathologist was Torres, the younger brother of Fernando, and standing beside him was an older bearded man hugging a large black container of some kind. The pathologist pulled back the sheet to reveal the tattooed face and head of Fernando.

'Let me see all of him,' said Torres.

The pathologist removed the sheet in a flourish to reveal the artwork in its supine aspect. The bearded man took a step forward and looked intently at the junctures of the body.

After a respectful silence, Torres said, 'I wish to make use of his organs.'

The pathologist made an amused expression and replied, 'He's been dead three days, and none of the organs are usable for transplant anymore.'

'There's one,' said Torres.

Immediately the pathologist understood what was going on and he looked more closely at the bearded man, who was still studying the cadaver and appeared to be making some complex calculations in his head.

'You know who this is?' asked Torres.

'Of course I do,' answered the pathologist. 'Fernando is – was – world-famous. These tattoos must rival the Mona Lisa in terms of familiarity.'

'Exactly. As Fernando's brother, I can't allow such a beautiful work of art to disappear from the world.'

The pathologist silently studied the two men before he said, 'Beautiful. And undoubtedly valuable.' He made a quick calculation before continuing. 'I'm afraid certain protocols have to be followed before any organs can be donated to patients on a waiting list. And if my guess is correct, in this case, there will be no waiting list so the difficulties in securing a transfer will be compounded – it could take weeks to sort out. You'll have to come back with the necessary paperwork.'

'I already have the paperwork,' said Torres as he put his hand into the inside of his jacket and pulled out a brown envelope that bulged with volume.

The pathologist adopted a poker face and said, 'And what does your paperwork say?'

Torres looked at the envelope and pretended to read it: 'It says, "ten thousand dollars".'

The pathologist thought for a moment and said, 'As the brother of Fernando, I'm sure you will eventually get all the necessary permissions to take possession of the body but by that time even the organ of the skin could deteriorate further... It would be a shame to see such beautiful work spoil.'

Torres couldn't disguise his annoyed expression and replied, 'What other paperwork am I missing?'

The pathologist said, 'A duplicate is needed, then all will be in order.'

Torres said, 'I don't have a duplicate with me and I was hoping to have the organ today.'

The pathologist cut to the chase: 'Give me the original document and your – friend here can do what he needs to do. I'll even allow him to use my blades. That insulated bag isn't really adequate for your needs. Once you've removed the organ I will store it here for you in ideal conditions. You can then bring me the duplicate document tomorrow and I'll arrange for a blood wagon to transport your organ to wherever it needs to go next. How does that sound?'

A little too quickly, Torres said, 'Deal,' and the pathologist realized he'd given in too cheaply. Still, he was in novel territory and twenty thousand dollars would still make a decent deposit on a nice boat.

'Good. Bring that gurney over and we'll get the body onto the dissecting table.'

The bearded man's face brightened with excitement. As a taxidermist, he'd never had the opportunity to flay a human being before and he imagined he was experiencing the same excitement that Michelangelo or Da Vinci must have felt when he was about to dissect his first human corpse in the dead of night. After Torres had located him as the most expert taxidermist in the area and explained to him what he was after, he'd carefully studied which incisions he would need to make and where so that the least interference was made with the artwork, and he was now confident he could preserve the beauty of the tattoos.

*

Many months later, a prestigious gallery in New York put on display its latest acquisition, bought for an undisclosed sum of money from an undisclosed dealer. The piece was a life-size mannequin of a human form that was exquisitely covered with the entire skin of Fernando. The head had glass eyes, and to the viewer, Fernando was still exhibiting himself, except now he was permanently in one place and immobile, so the tattoos lost one element of their beauty. The preservation process that the taxidermist had used however was kind enough to allow the unusual colours to remain and there was enough about the exhibit to excite genuine emotion.

The response from the public was mixed. Some were appalled at the idea that a dead person could be put on display like a work of art – especially as the rendition was so lifelike. Those who normally expressed no interest in art however were morbidly curious and were prepared to pay the entrance fee to get a glimpse of something that had previously been out of their reach. It was like the next step up from waxworks: instead of a facsimile, here was the actual skin of the celebrity – and what a skin! For the first time in their lives many people started to appreciate art; the mastery of line was unquestionable and the unusual iridescent colours were a scientific marvel to behold. The public flocked to the gallery, as they would have done in the past to a freak show.

The art establishment élite were ambivalent about this interest from the common public: they imagined the public did view it as a freak show but at the same time they rejoiced in the new era of art that would soon dawn in their lifetime. It was true, a genius like Jean-Michel wouldn't appear again for a very long time, if ever, but if new artists became interested in the tattoo legacy he'd left behind, great works would surely follow – and Bertram still held the patents for the special colours.

This new development had a devastating effect on the two remaining living artworks left in the world: they realized they had effectively become immortal. Not only had their celebrity status gone off the scale with the death of Jean-Michel but now that Fernando was a work of art in a prestigious gallery, their futures were mapped out for them: on their deaths, they too would be skinned and preserved and put on display in an art gallery. And they would remain like that for centuries to come.

This was especially intolerable for The End. Each day she would look at herself in the mirror and consider her body. The beauty of the tattoos was undeniable – the veins of gold running along her limbs, intertwining with the complex patterns of shimmering colours. Then she would look closer, at the shape of her breasts and the firmness of her muscles. At her current age, and with the workout regime she imposed upon herself, she was at the height of her beauty. Another ten years however and her breasts would begin to sag, the skin would dry and become less elastic. She was a work of art and her skin would be put on display for the appreciation of millions of people for centuries to come – how did she want to be remembered?

Maybe it would be better to die young.

The burden of this thought was intolerable enough but the genius of Jean-Michel was not yet finished and his final stroke of brilliance was still to be revealed.

The attendants in the New York gallery noticed it first. Over time they observed how certain parts of Fernando's tattoos were fading dramatically. And then they noticed some new lines emerging from the skin. How was that possible?

After several months the design on Fernando's body completely changed: a large part disappeared and new designs appeared to augment what was left. But here was the shock: the new design was so obscene that the gallery was forced to remove the exhibit. Investigations surmised that it was a grand joke played by Jean-Michel. He had anticipated this move by the art market to preserve his work and, to mock them, he'd devised special inks that were invisible in the skin but would become visible when certain chemicals used in taxidermy were applied to them. Similarly, he'd devised some colours to do the opposite – disappear when affected by certain chemicals. This was even better than the grand joke played by Michelangelo on his patrons when he painted God touching the hand of Adam on the Sistine Chapel ceiling. Michelangelo painted it in such a way that it represented the cross section of a human head and brain. Only someone else who had dissected a human head would make the connection. Michelangelo's criminal act was in full view for all to see throughout history.

Now the two living artworks were under intolerable pressure. The media speculated on whether Jean-Michel had played similar jokes with their tattoos, and an entire industry sprang up with websites suggesting alternate designs that might appear once the skins had been preserved.

Each day, the two living artworks would look at themselves in the mirror and ask themselves, 'What joke do I hide?'

Only death and acid would provide the answer.

The Trophy Hunters

The day's hunt had gone badly. All they saw were some herons and a dik-dik. Wayne managed to bring down the dik-dik with his crossbow and Lance blasted a couple of the birds with his rifle.

Dirk felt the tension from his clients: when you pay tens of thousands of dollars to go on a hunt you expect to kill more than tiny antelope and a few birds. But if the game isn't there, you can't just invent it.

The sun had already set and Kangwe had prepared the camp for the night. The hunters sat around a fire that crackled and spat occasionally.

'So, Dirk, what's your opinion on the most dangerous game in Africa? Buffalo or elephant?'

The question came from Lance, a huge Texan whose obese body didn't so much sit in the folding chair as spill over it like an overheated pudding. Sitting alongside him was Wayne, another American whose wire-and-whipcord frame made him look like the uninflated version of Lance.

Dirk observed his two clients by the light from the campfire and from a nearby hurricane lamp set on a table. Bottles of liquor also stood on the table and moths circled them like drunks looking for the entrance to a bar. He scratched his week-old beard and prepared to deliver his well-rehearsed answer when Kangwe surprised the trio by approaching them silently out of the darkness from the direction of the parked vehicles. As the native tracker it was his habit to move about silently, and his ebony-coloured skin aided his sudden, ghost-like appearance out of the night. He was carrying three empty glasses that he handed to the men in turn.

'What's your poison, gentlemen?' he asked.

Dirk said, 'I think we'll all have the bourbon, please, Kangwe.'

'Not for me, I'll have beer,' said Lance.

'Yes, boss.' Kangwe went to the table and by the light of the hurricane lamp selected an unopened bottle of Wild Turkey bourbon and a six-pack of Budweiser. After handing these out he said to Dirk, 'If that's all, boss, I'll go and prepare the food.'

'Yep, that's fine. I'll shout you if we need anything.'

Kangwe silently melted into the night in the direction from which he had come.

'If we can't kill any big game let's kill some brain cells, eh?' said Wayne as he cracked open the bottle and offered to pour some into Dirk's glass. Dirk reached out his arm and Wayne poured a good inch of the liquid into his tumbler before doing the same with his own. Lance peeled the ring-pull off a can and threw it onto the floor.

'To our good health,' said Wayne smiling broadly – his perfect set of teeth advertizing the impressive skills of his dentist.

The three men raised their drinks before swallowing a mouthful. All except Lance, who kept on glugging at his can until it was empty. No sooner was it emptied than he threw it onto the floor and pulled off another can from the webbing.

'Where was I?' asked Dirk. 'Ah, yes, the most dangerous game… I would say an elephant in must. The unpredictability and fury of these giants is something to behold. I was on this hunt once with an American client. We were tracking this bull – a good eleven tons of him – and as we got close Kangwe could see he was in must so I told Mister G we needed to approach with extreme caution, but he couldn't wait to get a good look at the magnificent ivory he was going to bag for himself and he

124

raced ahead. It wasn't long before the bull noticed him and charged. Mr G was extremely lucky I had my rifle cocked and loaded because I managed to get a shot off that stopped the bull in its tracks. Mr G then unloaded his rifle into him. I don't think he fully appreciated how lucky he was because afterwards he just complained about not being the one to fire the killing shot.'

Wayne said, 'Mister G? That wouldn't be Glen Gearheart, would it? That sounds like the kind of stupid stunt he'd pull.'

Dirk replied, 'You know him?'

'I knew him. He's dead now.'

'Oh, I didn't know that. He wasn't killed during a hunt, was he?'

'No, that's the weird thing,' Wayne said. 'He committed suicide – at least that's what the coroner's report said.'

'Suicide!' Dirk shouted. 'No way! My reading of that egomaniac told me he'd be the last man on earth to consider that form of exit.'

'Yeah, I must admit I was shocked myself when I heard it.'

Dirk took a sip of his drink and looked puzzled. 'Actually, that reminds me. A couple of my old clients passed away recently and one of them died from suicide too. At least that was the official explanation, but I had a few email exchanges with his widow and she didn't believe it. She told me he had nothing troubling him and would never take his own life. I know a lot of suicides are out of the blue but I believed her. From what I knew of him he was rock solid.'

'You said another client of yours died recently,' Lance said. 'What was the cause of death there?'

'Don't worry, it wasn't suicide, it was food poisoning. Well, poisoning of some kind. The report couldn't be sure, but as far as anyone could tell, he didn't have any enemies. Even his wife liked him.'

Lance threw another empty can onto the ground before grabbing a full one and said, 'Did you hear about Boris Shevchenko?'

'What about him?' Dirk said. 'I know he's a big hunter but he never responded to any of my mail outs to him offering my services as a guide.'

'He's dead too – poisoned.'

The two men looked at Lance. The only sounds were the crackling of the fire and the *tink* of beetles flying into the glass of the hurricane lamp.

Lance continued: 'I read about it in *Hunter* magazine, there was an obituary. Then a friend of mine who has business dealings in Russia told me a bit more about the case. Apparently the poisoning was suspicious and the authorities were leaving the case open pending further enquiries. Boris was a high flyer so he could have had a few enemies. My friend told this one weird bit of gossip though: as the authorities checked his movements they looked at his last hunt and all the people who were on it. There was this one guy they couldn't trace. He bought onto the safari late using cash. Nobody knew anything about this hunter, so the police want to talk to him.'

There was a loud *chink* sound as Wayne refilled his glass from the bottle of bourbon. He held it up to Dirk in a questioning action and Dirk held his glass out to have it refreshed.

'What, they think this mysterious hunter might be a killer or something?' asked Dirk.

Lance burped loudly before he said, 'He's a 'line of enquiry', as they say in copland.'

'Boris had a huge number of trophies, he was a prolific hunter,' added Wayne. 'I suppose...' He

126

suddenly started to laugh as a thought struck him. 'I suppose he would have made a good trophy himself for a hunter of hunters.'

'Now there's an idea,' said Lance. 'Hunting people. There's no shortage of that kind of game in this part of the world. I wonder how much sport they'd provide?'

'Well, there are people about you might be able to ask personally,' said Dirk. The statement hung in the warm air like the smell of cordite.

The other two men looked at Dirk as though trying to discern if he was joking or not. His expression suggested he wasn't.

'What d'ya mean?' asked Wayne as he brought the glass to his lips.

Dirk said, 'I heard these stories about the Angolan civil war – back in the Seventies. Lots of mercenaries were involved in that conflict and discipline was a bitch – people shooting their own side, desertions, massacres, that sort of thing. Towards the end of the fighting there were lots of refugees out in the bush trying to get to South Africa and Namibia. I heard some mercenaries went out hunting 'em for sport. These mercenaries could still be alive today.'

There was a sound of a can being crushed as Lance clenched his fist and said, 'So there are people around who've had the privilege of hunting humans. I'd love to try that sort of game. But what if you get a taste for it and find you don't want to stop doing it? That must be a real bummer.'

'Hey, what if one of these mercenaries was this guy on the safari with Boris?' slurred Wayne. 'Maybe he did it to continue to hunt people but he's chosen us hunters because we're the hardest to kill and the smartest game on the fucking savannah!'

'I'd like to see him hunt me,' said Lance. 'I'd spot him for sure and I'd crush him like this can.' He tossed the mangled can on the ground and reached for the last full one of the six-pack.

'But what if the killer was a sneaky bastard? You know, found other ways of killing his game,' Wayne said, now pointing his finger at nothing in particular. 'I mean, Boris was poisoned *after* the safari...' Then he raised another issue: 'Why haven't the police taken an interest? I haven't heard of any reports mentioning a serial killer targeting trophy hunters in any news I've seen – have you?'

'The police are too stupid to notice a pattern like that,' said Dirk. 'And think about it.' He took a big swig from his glass. 'If he's targeting people all over the world, who's going to join the dots? We're all hunters so we've got inside information about the people involved, we swap small talk. And look. We've only just noticed a possible connection between these suspicious deaths this evening. Maybe we're the first people to stumble onto a real-life killer of hunters.'

Wayne was deep in thought. He said, 'That makes sense – him being a hunter. He'd know how we think and what makes us tick. What if we've been on a hunt with him in the past and he's been studying us, getting intel on our lives, working out what we eat, what we drink?' He suddenly looked at his glass and at the liquid contained in it.

Dirk took up his train of thought: 'If he's a psychopath, you wouldn't be able tell that he'd been studying you coz they're brilliant at being sociable. I've read about 'em. They can show emotion but it's an act, the emotion isn't real. They use it to manipulate people.'

Dirk drained his glass and continued: 'They're also egomaniacs. They want people to know how fucking brilliant they are. So the problem he's got is that he's too good – we're probably the only people to have spotted the clues and seen some kind of spoor. According to all the info I've read, at some point he's going to escalate his MO until a cop or a reporter is going to recognize his work. It's not beyond the bounds of possibility that he might even kill on a safari and take down a hunter as they themselves are preparing to take down a wild animal.' He paused before he added, 'He might even be one of us.'

The three men looked at each other as if they'd simultaneously discovered one of them was a traitor. Out in the blackness of the night a far-off hyena yipped.

Lance suddenly made movements to stand up. After some effort he succeeded. 'I need a piss,' he said and staggered off towards the latrine area.

When he was gone Wayne said to Dirk in a hushed voice, 'Why is he drinking beer and not bourbon like us? You know, I'm starting to have a bad feelin' about this.'

Dirk knitted his brow. 'What are you sayin'?'

'I'm sayin' he could have put poison in the bottle.'

'But the bottle was capped. If he wanted to put poison in it how could he do that without breaking the seal?'

'I dunno, if he's a clever hunter he'd have figured something out to fool us! Or maybe he's gone to get a weapon now and he's going to shoot us while we're both unarmed. I've got lots of trophies back home, if he's gonna want anybody as a trophy it's gonna be me as I'm one of the best fucking hunters around.'

Dirk thought about this. 'I suppose if you were going to ambush prey, the best time to do it would be when they're not expecting it or they're incapacitated in some way.'

'I don't trust the bastard. I'm going to get my crossbow just in case he tries anything funny.'

Before Dirk could say anything, Wayne jumped out of his chair and headed towards his tent.

A minute later Lance returned from the latrine and appeared within the light of the campfire.

'Where's Wayne gone?' he asked.

Just then, in the darkness beyond the light, Wayne could be heard returning from his tent accompanied by the sound of machinery being manipulated. Then there was a small thud as Wayne's foot stubbed into a burrow. There was a 'Fuck!' followed by a larger thud as Wayne fell to the ground. Then there was a hissing sound.

Dirk saw Lance stagger back and the flesh around his chest rippled in short waves as the bolt slammed into him. The bolt completely disappeared into his bulk. He stood motionless for a second, a confused look on his face. The look reminded Dirk of so many elephants he'd seen after they'd been mortally wounded. There was that exquisite moment when the elephant tried to make sense of what was happening to it before it toppled to the ground in an ungainly heap.

Lance fell straight backwards. As he hit the ground a donut-shaped cloud of dust erupted around him.

That's when Kangwe appeared and announced dinner was ready.

Mr Goole

Notes of Mr Goole: Patient 'Harriet'

Thursday, October 3rd 11 a.m.

Patient Harriet came to my office this morning for a consultation. She is a smart, attractive woman aged about fifty, married with one child. She told me about her phobia with mobile phones that, she claims, began recently. She can't own one at all and is terrified of other people's going off around her. A close friend of hers referred her to me.

I accepted her as my patient and told her to return next week.

Thursday, October 10th 11 a.m.

Harriet turned up for our appointment seemingly dressed in exactly the same clothes as last week – a turquoise polo-necked top, camel-haired coat and a pair of red shoes. I only remember the outfit because it was so striking. This could be sheer coincidence or my memory is playing tricks on me but as soon as she walked into my office it struck me as being odd. I note it here as it may become significant as the treatments continue.

We talked generally about her phobia, when it manifests and how she reacts physically when an incident occurs (panic attacks). My initial thoughts were that she is scared of the speed of change in technology; however, as we continued talking it became apparent that she is an intelligent woman who embraces new technology, as she uses computers at home and owns a tablet.

This first session didn't produce any clear idea of where the real problem lies or what kind of treatment would be suitable. She agreed to come back next week.

Thursday, October 17th 11 a.m.
After making a note of the clothes she wore last week I can confirm she wore the same clothes at this session. Why? What can I read from this? They are well-tailored clothes and she has paid my invoices promptly so I can only conclude it is a deliberate choice of hers to wear these clothes and nothing to do with lack of funds.

She surprised me in the session by asking me if I would hypnotize her as part of the therapy. This is unusual. It is always me who initiates the idea after I've divined that the patient is burying something traumatic deep inside their memory. I'm not even sure if she's susceptible to hypnosis. I asked her why she thought this was a good idea. She told me that she thought something might 'come out' during the hypnosis. I was troubled by this suggestion, as she was pre-empting my diagnostic assessment of the situation. It felt like she was steering the direction of the analysis, not me, but my curiosity was sufficiently aroused to overcome any doubts I might have had about the possible dangers. We agreed that at the next session I would hypnotize her.

Thursday, October 24th 11 a.m.
Harriet failed to appear at the allotted time. I'm wondering if she's had second thoughts about the hypnosis. I know I have. I don't think it's the right time in the treatment process to attempt it.

Friday, October 25th
Harriet dropped by my office today when I was out and left a hand-written note. She apologized for the no-show

132

and asked if she could attend at the usual time next week. I emailed her to confirm the appointment, and reassured her that we don't need to go down the hypnosis avenue if she doesn't want to.

Thursday, October 31st 11 a.m.

Astonishing! I have never experienced anything like the session that just happened.

Harriet arrived early for her session and seemed overly anxious to get on with it. She was wearing exactly the same clothes as on all previous occasions and I still have no insight as to what this might mean. I put her in the comfy chair and began the hypnosis procedure. She went under very quickly. I asked her to tell me her name and date of birth, etc. She answered these questions correctly and in her normal voice but when I began to probe her past with more intimate questions her voice changed dramatically. It took on a deeper tone and some of the inflexions in the words vaguely reminded me of someone I know. It was as if she were trying to do a bad impression of this person – who did it remind me of?

Then Harriet stopped being the passive interviewee in the session and started to ask me questions. Her tone was calm but firm. Such was the dramatic change in her voice that I felt compelled to make sure 'Harriet' was okay.

'I'm sensing a change in your voice, Harriet. Is that still you talking?' I asked.

'No, Peter, Harriet is just a messenger. *I* wanted to talk with you.'

During my training I'd read about remarkable cases where patients undergo personality changes and then come out with astonishing statements or voices but I always thought these reports might be somewhat exaggerated by an overexcited psychiatrist caught up in the heat of the moment. But now, here I was with exactly the same scenario. In the case studies I'd read, the psychiatrist always played along with the patient and no harm was ultimately caused. Knowing this didn't calm my growing anxiety. I tried to find my new role in the drama that was unfolding before me – Harriet was either a genuine complex case of schizophrenia or a brilliant actor. Either way, goose bumps appeared on my exposed flesh. (I also have to confess that at the same time I couldn't help egotistically thinking that this case could be a high point of my career.)

'If you're not Harriet, then who are you?'

'Peter, it's me, Mummy.'

My pen fell from my fingers. Even after preparing myself for an unexpected turn of events this statement still caught me unawares and I could feel the heat building up in my body. It was as if Harriet was now revealing that she knew more about psychiatry than I did and was demonstrating exactly how to exploit a deep sense of guilt in a personality.

My default action in such situations is to revert to logic and to rationalize as much as I can. Firstly, my mother is still alive and has my telephone number so she can easily reach me if she wants to – no need to go to all the trouble of employing a medium. Why is this person pretending to represent my mother? Who's put her up to it? What's in it for her? I needed to clarify the situation.

'Let me make sure I understand this correctly, Harriet; you're saying you are not the real patient here, you are simply carrying a message from someone who claims to be my mother? Have I got his right?'

'Yes, Peter. You were always good at working things out, you've got the gist of it.'

Still relying on my default first line of defence, I thought to test Harriet about her assertion. If I asked her something specific about my life and she couldn't answer it correctly I could reassure myself that she was improvising this conversation. I had to quickly think of something to ask her that she couldn't have discovered by doing a recent social media search on my background.

'So you remember that day I fell off my bike when I was five, and broke my wrist? Can you tell me about that?'

'It was such a glorious day in summer, we'd all gone to Beaumont Park to enjoy the duck pond and gardens. You were having such a wonderful time on your bike, you were so proud you could ride it without stabilizers and you zoomed around in the wide-open spaces. You were so excited you forgot to look where you were going and hit a tree. I was so worried about you afterwards, Peter, that I put the stabilizers back on your bike. You were furious.'

Impossible! Only an intimate of the family would know this anecdote. Either Harriet had done her research thoroughly or a supernatural phenomenon of some kind was being demonstrated right in front of my eyes. I had been reluctant at first to respond to the voice as if it were my mother talking – it could all still be a charade – but after this revelation of family knowledge I sensed great progress would be made if I were to do so. Therefore, I composed myself and continued the conversation.

'But Mummy, you're still alive. Why don't you simply call me and speak to me that way?'

'Don't you remember, darling? I have a fear of telephones now.'

'Ah, of course! And a fear of mobile phones specifically?'

'Yes.'

'Mummy, are you and Harriet related in some way?'

'Peter, is that really you? It's so good to feel your presence again. I've missed you so much.'

Here, Harriet took several quick, shallow breaths and her voice became loaded with such emotion that I doubted any actor could achieve that level of pathos. I began to feel decidedly uneasy about the situation. I was, now, way out of my depth. None of my training and experience was helping me anymore. I pressed on.

'Mummy, are you wanting to tell me something in particular? Has something happened?'

'The telephone call…'

'You got an important telephone call, is that it? When did you get this call?'

'A long time ago. Peter, I know you're still here, still listening to me. I *know* it.'

'Tell me about the telephone call, Mummy. Who telephoned you?'

'God, no, not the telephone call. That horrible, horrible day.'

'Who telephoned you? Was it me? Was it Daddy?'

'I didn't know him, Peter. He had a calm voice. I've not spoken to him since.'

'What did this man say to you? It was something bad, wasn't it? Can you tell me what this man said, Mummy?'

Harriet shuddered uncontrollably at this point and tears tumbled down her powdered cheeks. It took her a minute or two to recover her composure.

She continued: 'He said a part of me was missing, that it was broken and needed to be fixed. He said I should go to the hospital.'

'Are you ill, Mummy? Was it a doctor who diagnosed something wrong with you? Why didn't you tell me about this when I last saw you…?'

As I said this it suddenly dawned on me that I couldn't remember the last time I had seen my mother. When was it?

'I had to go to the hospital. I had to go quickly, it was an emergency. I'm so sorry, Peter.'

'Sorry for what, Mummy? What happened at the hospital? What was wrong with you?'

'They said they didn't know. So little is known. I had to wait.'

'Were you waiting to see a specialist? Is that it? Are you waiting for a cure?'

'Yes! Yes! A cure!'

I was frightened now and I felt a huge impulse to break off the session and telephone my mother to make sure she was all right. At the back of my mind I knew this was superstitious nonsense. I'm an avowed rationalist but at that moment I got such a sense of foreboding and terror that I just wanted to run out of the room. As strong as the impulse was to get out my phone and call my mother, my responsibility was with the patient in front of me, so I stayed with her.

'All right, Mummy, let's see if I can help. Tell me, what disease did the doctors say you had?'

'They said I had a broken heart.'

A broken heart? This didn't make sense. In fact, very little was making sense now. I pieced together the facts I had at my disposal: This strange woman makes herself my patient, attends every session without ever changing her clothes and now pretends to be a conduit to my mother with knowledge of anecdotes that only my immediate family would know. What the hell was going on?

'Mummy, why do you have a broken heart?'

'The telephone call, Peter. It was about you.'

I froze. Was this about transference? It's far too early in the treatment for that. None of my training as a psychiatrist had prepared me for such a scenario. I was losing control of the situation – I could feel it. Not only that but I was also losing my ability to rationalize my thoughts. The more I analyzed the small details of our meetings, the more bizarre they appeared when I applied time and logic to them. I sensed she was analyzing me, probing me, waiting for me to become ready – ready for what? She was testing the ground, gently tamping the thin meniscus of reality to see if it was strong enough to bear the weight of her next sentence. My years of training had alerted me to be on my guard for such significant moments. Harriet was about to drop a psychological bombshell, I knew it – she was going to expose the raw and ghastly trauma that had started off this drama.

'Go on, Mummy.'

'The faceless man at the other end of the telephone, the one with the calm voice, he told me there was an accident. You were on your way to the hospital. You were going to start your new job there as a consultant psychiatrist. You were so happy, so excited. Your future was a wide-open space. You were on your bicycle again, how you loved to cycle... but you were on the road. Then the speeding car appeared from round the corner...'

Suddenly time and space begin to smear and spin into a distorted image. The spinning speeds up until only a vortex of colour and lights remains, and then they too get sucked into a singularity. Harriet, me, the room – my fear, all vanish.

*

At that moment, a patient in Addenbrooke's hospital in Cambridge opens his eyes for the first time in six months and his ever-present mother, dressed in a turquoise polo-necked top and red shoes, frantically shouts for a nurse.

For Sale, Sex Robot, Hardly Used

The shop exterior was designed with a deliberate Victorian look: an old-fashioned, black gas-lamp flickered above the door. As far as Randy could tell, the naked flame inside the glass was authentic, though he couldn't remember the last time he saw an actual flame or indeed whether he'd ever seen one. Most of his information about the past came from virtual reality experiences.

He pushed open the door, inset with panes of blistered-glass, and an old-fashioned bell tinkled above his head. The inside of the shop, however, abandoned the Victorian theme. It was modern with clean lines, and concealed lighting with such a high lumen level that everything around him looked slightly surreal.

Randy got the immediate impression that the shop was filled with customers – male, female, old, young, fat, short. But as no one was moving he soon realized these were the products. He stopped at the first person he encountered and studied the face closely. It was a young woman around twenty years old, dressed in tight-fitting clothing that showed off her curvaceous figure. He inspected her lips: they were puckered and seductively red. He put a finger on the bottom lip and pressed it speculatively: it was soft to the touch but not wet. A mild alarm sounded from her mouth.

'We ask that the customers don't touch the merchandise without permission.'

The voice came from the other end of the shop. A man stood behind the counter. He was young, clean-shaven, handsome and dressed in a black polo-necked jumper. 'Are you looking for anything in particular, sir?'

Randy replied in his Southern drawl, 'I am. How much is this one?'

The man emerged from behind the counter and walked up to Randy. The shop assistant was so short that Randy felt he was dealing with a child.

'Oh, she's very pretty, isn't she?' said the assistant. 'I'd go for her myself. She can perform all sorts of other functions—'

'How much?' asked Randy.

'Fifty thousand tokens,' answered the assistant. 'We have easy payment facilities if—'

'That's too much. What else you got?'

'Is it a sex partner you're after?'

'Yep.' Randy's fleshy cheeks wobbled when he snapped his jaw shut.

'And what is your budget?'

'Put it this way, it ain't fifty thousand.'

'Hmm.' The assistant turned on his heel. 'Follow me, sir. I'll show you the items we have at the lower end of our price range.' He walked to a glass cabinet that contained various body parts and opened the door. He took down a naked foot, terminated just above the ankle but finished off smoothly with unblemished skin, and handed it to Randy. It was an elegant female foot. The toenails were painted bright red. He toyed with the toes and checked their pliability. They responded in a perfectly human way.

'When turned on, the foot heats up to body temperature,' the assistant purred. 'It has a sweat facility too that you can control, so you can regulate the slickness.'

Randy rested the sole of the foot on his ample cheek and rubbed gently. It felt good; tactile and velvety, like a baby's skin. 'How much?' he asked.

'Special offer just for today, only nine thousand tokens, down from ten.'

Randy handed the foot back abruptly to the assistant without looking at him and said, 'I hope there's a discount for a pair. Not that I'm in the market for feet.' Before the assistant could answer Randy continued: 'What else you got? Lemme see that head.'

The assistant carefully put the foot back in the cabinet then produced the head of a woman with blue-black hair designed to fall over one of her eyes. Her face looked identical to the product Randy had first encountered in the shop. Randy held the head between his hands and looked her full in the face. She had her eyes closed and her mouth slightly open.

'She comes with voice control,' the assistant explained, 'so you can regulate the hydraulic pressure of the mouth.'

Randy cocked his head from side to side before handing the head back. 'I really want the full model, not just bits of one. Are you sure you don't have anything more... affordable?'

The assistant studied Randy to assess his likely profile: he was dressed in combat fatigues that didn't disguise his obesity, his attitude was cocky, which suggested a moneyed background, but he was also gauche, which suggested a lack of privilege. The assistant came to a decision.

'Well, if you're not too choosy, we do have something second-hand – a complete model.'

Randy jerked his head to look at the assistant. 'So that would be a hell of a lot cheaper?'

The assistant was circumspect: 'It would allow me some room to negotiate,' he responded.

'Okay, lemme see it. I can put up with second-hand.'

The assistant closed the glass cabinet and moved to the back of the shop to a plain, unsigned door.

'This way,' he said. He opened the door into a dingy storeroom. The lights came on as soon as they detected the assistant, and Randy followed him in.

In a corner of the room, amidst various boxes and piles of clothing, he saw her: a little girl sitting on the floor with her hands on her knees and her head resting against the wall. She looked about five years old.

'This is Angie,' the assistant said. 'At least, that's what the previous owner called her. You can obviously change that to whatever pet name you like.'

Angie was in a floral dress and had a pink bow in her mousy hair. She was designed to look like an archetypal Western girl from the early 2000s. To Randy's eye she looked to be in good condition, practically new.

'She looks all right,' he said 'Wake her up for me.'

The assistant pulled out a device from his pocket and wanded it over her, then said, 'Yes, there's enough charge,' and motioned another instruction on the device.

The girl stirred. Her eyelids fluttered open and her head came upright. She looked around her, wide-eyed, a confused expression on her face (*Nice touch!* thought Randy) then she looked at Randy and smiled sweetly.

'Say "hello",' said the assistant to Randy. 'Use her pet name.'

'Hello, Angie.'

Angie spoke with a singsong quality to her voice: 'Hello, mister. I'm lost and I can't find my mommy. Will you help me?'

The effect was instantaneous and Randy felt heat rising in his loins. She was adorable.

Randy had to tear his gaze away from Angie. 'Why did the previous owner trade her in?'

The assistant raised his eyebrows and shrugged his shoulders. 'He claimed he became *woke* and couldn't bear to use her anymore. It sometimes happens when the models are this good.'

Randy looked at Angie again, this time with hardness in his eyes. 'Does she scream?' he asked.

The assistant moved closer and swung a foot viciously at the girl's ankle. Angie screamed in pain and started to sob.

'Wow. Tears, as well. Impressive.'

'Oh, this model is a classic,' the assistant said. 'Her distress responds proportionally to your own excitement, so the more excited you become the more her screams increase in volume until she becomes hysterical. And she can speak in several languages and beg for mercy in a religion of your choice. So if you want to prolong your pleasure you can have her calling for God or reciting prayers and psalms of whichever faith you choose.'

'Oh, that's sweet. I've just done a virtual tour of some rag-head country and I liked the way the civilians begged out stuff in Arabic before I blew their heads off.'

'Ah, you're a war games player too?'

Randy held out his arms to indicate his combat fatigues. 'Can't you tell? I play a lot – perhaps too much. Each session costs a fortune in tokens. That's why I need to budget with my choice of toy. You done the war games yourself?'

'Sure have.'

'Awesome! I was amazed the first time I played at how all the blood and guts gets your pecker up. I really wanted to rape one of the women during the game but they don't let ya, you can only blow their heads off.'

'Ah, so that's why you want a playmate?'

'Yeah. Although it's gonna spoil the fun, having all the carnage in the war games and then having to wait until I get home before I can satisfy myself.'

The assistant sympathized: 'That's governments interfering with our individual freedoms for you. Legislation that restricts our own personal pleasure.'

'You betcha!' Randy joined in. 'An' I mean, it's all private stuff in our own homes and none of their goddam business. No one gets hurt so where's the problem...?'

'Absolutely. They're your tokens, you should be free to do what you want with them so long as it doesn't bother anyone else.'

Randy looked at the assistant with his jaw thrust out and gave a little nod. The gesture told the assistant that Randy liked the comment. And his supposition was confirmed when Randy said, 'I've got twenty-five K. That's a good price for her.'

The assistant frowned. 'I know she's second-hand but you've seen how beautifully she behaves. And I'm sure once you use her you'll appreciate all the extras such as the screaming and the beseeching for her god.' He paused, thinking. 'I can't let her go for anything less than thirty-five thousand tokens.'

Randy looked at the girl, who was now rubbing her leg and sobbing pitifully. Her back shook violently with each sob. The attention to detail was irresistible. He wanted her – badly.

'I might be able to stretch to thirty K, but it's gonna hurt me.' He looked at the assistant as if needing help. The assistant responded.

'Look, I like you; you're a straight-up guy. I'll let you have her for thirty-two thousand tokens and I'll give you an easy payment plan spread over the long term so you shouldn't feel the pain too much. How does that sound?'

Randy stared at the girl again, still undecided.

In his pocket, the assistant discreetly operated the remote. The girl looked at Randy and sobbed: 'Please don't hurt me, please, mister.'

'Goddamn it! You've just got yourself a deal.' Randy stuck his fist out to the assistant, unable to tear his eyes away from the girl. The assistant indicated the deal was sealed by touching Randy's fist with his own.

Later, once the token checks had been done and the deal block-chained, the smiling assistant watched Randy walk to the door of the shop holding Angie's hand. Her other arm was clutching a teddy bear to her little chest. The bear was a bit of upselling that the assistant had done - Angie was programmed to become distraught if she was unable to find it.

Still smiling, the assistant watched them go out the door then walked back to his station behind the counter, where he plugged himself into the charger and resumed his usual waiting position, ready for the next customer.

The Time Traveller

The kitchen looked tidy enough. She checked the microwave oven. Empty. Good. She was afraid she was going to find a pair of shoes in there one day, or something equally inedible.

The work surfaces were free of crumbs and stains. At least the carers seemed to be doing their job properly.

She went to the sink to inspect what might be in it and her heart sank. In the orange plastic bowl sat a wood-cased mantelpiece clock. It was half submerged in foamy water. He must have been trying to clean it. As she glanced out of the window she caught sight of him – her dad.

He had his back to her and was gingerly digging a hole in the garden. His frail body working the spade with a slow, methodical determination.

Relieved that she'd located him, she went outside. From where she stood on the lawn she could see he had been busy. In the area of the garden where they used to bury all the family pets were several shallow holes with untidy mounds of fresh earth next to them.

'Dad?'

He continued to work the spade, oblivious to her voice. She walked across the lawn until she stood next to him. He looked up. A momentary fog of confusion drifted over his eyes. He greeted her with a nod then resumed his gentle digging.

She studied him for signs of any serious decline. He was clean-shaven today. That was a good indication that he still cared about his appearance. He was reasonably dressed too, although he was using his pyjama top as a shirt – its generous fitting made it bunch out from underneath the threadbare jumper he'd tucked into his trousers. She noticed on his left wrist he was wearing two watches.

'What are you doing, Dad? You never leave the house so what's got into you?'

'It's time to dig. I made a promise to myself. I nearly forgot.'

His broad smile exposed the gap in his front teeth. A legacy of a horse-riding accident decades ago. These days he never wore his plate.

'Why is it time to dig? Are you going to plant some vegetables now that it's spring?'

His expression changed to one of concern. 'You know your mother's died, don't you?'

'Yes, Dad, I know. Mum died months ago. Why are you digging the holes in the garden?'

A happy expression returned to his face. 'I'm going to travel through time at last. The machine is here, in the Garden of Eden.' And he continued to dig.

As children they'd called this patch of the garden the Garden of Eden. She could see no old bones that might belong to the many pets they'd buried here. No doubt they were much deeper than her dad could manage to dig today. 'So you're going to travel through time, are you? What date are you going to end up in?'

He looked at the watches on his wrist. She noticed they showed different times. 'You're too young to appreciate this but time isn't real – look.' He showed her the watch faces. 'Here, the time might be five o'clock but in another part of the world it would be midnight. How is that possible? The only time that matters is right now. But that doesn't mean we can't travel through time.' He returned to his digging, stopped suddenly and turned to her. 'You know your mother's died, don't you?'

'Yes, Dad, I know.'

He looked relieved, as if he'd just discharged an important duty, then changed the subject. 'What are you going to study when you get to university? You know how important an education is – to get ahead in this world you need an education.'

'I'm thinking of doing a PhD in physics.' She'd learned that it's best to go along with whatever he said. Any hint of contradiction and he would get frustrated to the point of violence. As she was now a forty-year-old teacher at a junior school, her university days were well and truly behind her.

'The sciences! Good. I've got a degree in science so we'd have one each. We could discuss the papers being published about new technological developments. Have you heard about the discovery of DNA? And look what science has given to everyone – the machines, the better health and now time travel!'

He returned to digging with renewed enthusiasm, lifting a small heap of soil onto the pile. A pungent smell of fecund earth filled her nostrils.

He did indeed have a degree in the sciences. His job had been as an electrical engineer with a nearby defence contractor and although he wasn't personally involved in any major developments, she remembered he always felt proud of his company for being at the forefront of new scientific breakthroughs. Nuclear physics particularly excited him. His old job had been his entire life. And now this house was his entire life, his entire world – he'd never lived anywhere else. As an only child he'd inherited the house from his parents when they both died in a car crash. Even when he'd attended university in the city he still lived here.

He lifted the spade as high as he could and brought it down with some effort, although the principal force behind the blade was still gravity. There was a metallic *CLUNK* as it bit into the soil.

'The treasure! I knew it,' he shouted. 'We can go forwards or we can go backwards in time. We can put all the pieces of the puzzle together again!'

She watched him with sudden interest. He appeared to have found something that existed outside of his imagination.

She watched him struggle for a couple of minutes trying to dig around the object but the earth was too compact and he made little progress so she went to the wooden garage and found a trowel.

'Here, Dad, let me help you.' She knelt down to dig more carefully around the object.

'Yes, yes, the machine is delicate and we need to be careful.'

She could see it was a tin of some kind. She had to put real effort into releasing the earth surrounding it.

Eventually she could lift the object out and bring it fully into the daylight. It was about the size of a small loaf of bread. After wiping most of the dirt off with her hands she could see the lettering on the tin more clearly and the word *Carr's* stood out in faded maroon ink. What could have once been black carpet tape sealing the lid crumbled away in scabby flakes.

'Blackie helped me bury it.' He held his hands out for the tin, the spade falling away by his side.

Blackie, a collie, was Dad's dog when he was a child. She remembered him always talking about Blackie, and despite the many dogs they'd kept over the years he remained the special one for Dad. He was the pet that taught Dad's young brain that life is only temporary and death permanent. Blackie was a terrible rite of passage.

He tried to open the tin but it was too rusted and his bony fingers couldn't produce the necessary grip. She took the tin from him and with much effort and sometimes using the trowel, she prised the lid off. Kneeling down on the lawn, she placed the tin in front of her. Her dad slowly eased himself onto the cool grass too, to get a closer look. Inside were newspaper cuttings, cinema ticket stubs and a wooden toy made from a cotton spool. There was also a black-and-white photograph of a collie dog. She took it out and handed it to him. At the bottom of the tin was a piece of paper. She lifted this out and delicately unfolded it.

It was a letter written in blue fountain-pen ink. A neat, immature handwriting filled the lined notepaper.

'It's some kind of letter. Do you want me to read it out?' Her dad had placed the photo of Blackie in front of him and was now reaching into the tin to pick out other objects.

'Yes, yes, read it,' he said as he arranged the objects.

She stood up to free her skirt – one she'd made herself – pulled out a pair of reading glasses from a pocket and started to read aloud.

'This is my time capsule with a message to my future self (or anyone else who might find it in case I'm living on the moon or somewhere). My science teacher, Mr Gordon, said I might find this experiment interesting. My name is Peter Mitchell and I am eleven years old. I am living in the year 1953 and I am so excited to be alive at this time. Science is going to make things bigger and better and who knows, we might even get to fly into space. I hope to study hard and pass all my exams so that one day I can work on the machines that will make everyone happier and healthier. The war years have been hard for us all but now we can buy sweets again and there is everything to look forward to. I want to be part of the team that builds this wonderful new future. I'm going to make a list of predictions here and my future self will look through my list of predictions and see if I was right about them.

'Hello, Peter! Let's see if we were right about the future...'

She looked down at her dad, astounded by both the find and his feat of remembering. From the shattered remains of his past he'd managed to unearth a shard of memory like a piece of pottery and visualize the world that the fragment told of.

Peter looked up at her with a beatific expression. He had surrounded himself with all the objects from the tin as if they were the controls of a fabulous time machine and she could almost see the child in him as he yelled, 'I've found him at last! I've found Blackie again. I knew time could be conquered.'

She had never seen him so happy – as if Blackie was really by his side, licking his hand. She had the sense that he had travelled back in time to a place in his memory that felt completely safe and familiar, to a world that made perfect sense to him.

Then, like a cloud passing over the sun, his expression changed and showed concern again as he was forced back into the present. She watched as he struggled to remember something, something important. His face brightened, and she knew it had come to him at last...

'You know your mother's died, don't you?'

Sobbing, she replied, 'Yes Dad, I know.'

Yorkshire Sculpture Park, October, 2018

The weather forecast was for a freakishly warm day with unbroken sunshine and, judging from business at the Yorkshire Sculpture Park car park that Wednesday morning, many of the visitors believed they were in for a cracking day.

Mitch had arranged to meet his friend Bill outside the gift shop entrance with the idea of spending a leisurely day walking around the splendid grounds of the park.

Mitch arrived first. He decided to wait just outside the entrance to the main building so that he could enjoy the sunshine. He sat on a bench opposite the car park and kept an eye out for Bill. He wasn't too concerned about keeping a constant look out because he was sure if he didn't see Bill, Bill would spot him. Mitch was not easily missed. He was a large man: six feet four inches tall and weighing nearly sixteen stones. He was dressed in a horizontally-striped, blue-and-white rugby shirt, salmon-pink trousers and light-brown deck shoes. His thick grey hair sprouted like unruly cauliflower on his head. A pair of tiny but expensive binoculars hung around his neck.

Within a couple of minutes he heard his name being called – Bill had arrived. Mitch turned and saw a man walking towards him who was wearing thick-framed dark glasses and a black Stetson hat. His most distinctive feature was his handlebar moustache: it grew so thickly on his upper lip that it seemed to flow out of his nostrils in a flood of bristles and could easily be mistaken for a fake one that he'd clipped to his nose. Mitch assumed that the moustache was carefully dyed every month because a sixty-year-old man sporting such uniformly black facial hair seemed unlikely. In their long friendship he'd never thought to ask him if he did dye it. Bill's black headgear was matched with a beautifully tailored black shirt, a black leather waistcoat, black jeans and black boots. A blood-red neckerchief set off the whole ensemble. All that he was missing to be the archetypal bad guy from a Western movie was a six-shooter hanging from his hip.

There was a firm handshake between the men; arthritis hadn't attacked either of their hands yet.

Mitch said, 'I suggest we go anti-clockwise today, just for the hell of it.' Bill shrugged his shoulders in a carefree manner and they commenced their walk around the park.

The first new piece of sculpture they encountered consisted of three piles of sandstone blocks, stacked in such a way as to form rectangular structures.

'Oh dear,' said Mitch.

'What's up?' asked Bill.

'I feel a rant coming on.'

The massive structures towered above them as the two men strolled around the artworks. Each block of stone varied from the size of a washing machine to a double bed. The stone was not worked in any way other than being cut roughly into rectangles by big machines and drills. The one response it did evoke in the men was a childish urge to climb the structures using the easy handholds and footholds offered by the gaps between the blocks, but a prominent sign instructed visitors to resist such a temptation and, just in case they couldn't read, a thin rope around the sculptures created a border of forbidden territory.

'Is this art?' asked Mitch.

Bill stroked his moustache in a dastardly manner. 'There's no such thing as art, as you well know, Mitch, only artists.'

'As a child I grew up near a sandstone quarry which I often explored on boring Sunday afternoons. This,' and he waved his arms vaguely at the blocks, 'could be lifted straight from that quarry. In fact, you'd get more appreciation of stone by standing at the foot of the rock-face in the quarry where they'd been cutting the slabs off than by standing in front of these things. What is this supposed to do for the viewer?'

Bill offered, 'Maybe the art is contained in putting the stone here in this open field miles away from any quarry and then stacking the blocks into a geometrical design.'

'Okay, but how is this different from standing at the foot of the cliffs on the Jurassic Coast with the sea behind you and observing all the different layers of rock? In fact, how is it any different from admiring a dry-stone wall? The exact same criteria apply: stones in a field, stacked geometrically in a pleasing pattern. The wall even has a bloody purpose!'

'So the wall can't be art then. Isn't it playing on the standing stones idea from ancient times? Shall we read the notes?' Bill looked around for the plaque or sign that would probably explain the inspiration for the piece. Or not.

'Sod that! You know my policy – if I have to read a great long thesis to understand what's going on, I'm not interested.' And as if to emphasize the point he cried, 'Come on, let's go!'

They walked up the gently sloping field towards the Long Gallery, discussing the state of modern art, when Mitch had a thought: 'I'm beginning to suspect that the human race is starting to outgrow the idea of art.'

Bill burst out laughing. 'You can't be serious,' he managed to say between guffaws. 'The human species is defined by its creativity. We're the only species that creates art.'

'I'm not denying that but what if art is becoming a useless appendage, like a human appendix? It would naturally atrophy and drop off. We're still evolving as a species - maybe art is at a transitional stage.'

'And what would it be transitioning into?'

'I'm not too sure. Into something more contemplative, more thoughtful. Like Zen.'

When they reached the Long Gallery there was another installation they hadn't seen before, erected on the grass bank by the corner of the building. It consisted of sheets of metal stacked up as you might find them in any steel fabrication warehouse run by a foreman with bad OCD.

'Oh dear,' said Mitch. This time Bill didn't ask what the problem was, he already knew. They had a look around the Long Gallery but Bill felt the need to hustle Mitch out of it as soon as possible as the artworks were having a deleterious effect on his mental health.

They walked up onto the ridge of the hill known as Oxley Bank that commanded a splendid view of the old Bretton Hall and the surrounding countryside. From one angle they could make out the M1 in the distance with ant-like vehicles crawling backwards and forwards along a black line in the landscape. Both men sat on the bench that had been positioned to take advantage of the vista and looked on in silence. Bill took off his Stetson, untied the red neckerchief from around his neck and wiped his sweating forehead with it. The climb and his black clothes in the burning sunshine had made him sweat profusely and his clothes felt uncomfortably clammy. Mitch peered through his binoculars at the horizon, at nothing in particular; he just liked the power of being able to see into the distance.

'Do you want to take a look?' he asked Bill.

'There's nothing much to see – the heat is making the horizon too fuzzy.' They both stared at the view in silence again. Mitch gave a satisfied sigh before he said, 'Beautiful. Let's continue.'

As they made their way through the trees along the ridge, Bill said, 'Hang on, I want to have a look at the Goldsworthy piece,' and he walked down a short little path that led to the boundary wall adjacent to a field. Jutting out from the wall was an enclosure built in the same style as the wall. When Mitch joined him and they looked over the enclosure wall they could see a deep pit about ten feet in depth and suspended in the void was a tree trunk lying horizontally. It was held up from the ground by being built into the surrounding stonework, as if it were growing through the walls in an unnatural manner. The piece was old now and the tree trunk was starting to rot heavily, which detracted from its weird configuration.

'Look,' said Mitch. 'Again, we can see this allusion to nature. I know Goldsworthy works with natural materials anyway but why do artists refer to the natural world? Is it because most people are becoming so divorced from nature that they need to be reminded of it?'

'It's funny,' said Bill. Mitch looked at Bill in an expectation of a conclusion to this statement but none came. Bill noticed Mitch's puzzled look and said, 'I mean, this configuration is like a funny joke, an elaborate joke that makes me think, *huh?*'

'I sometimes think that about life,' said Mitch.

They came to the end of the ridge and started the slow descent that led towards the lake. A familiar artwork greeted them in the trees: 'Speed Breakers' by Hemali Bhuta.

'Oh dear,' said Mitch.

Both men stared at the bronze tree roots poking out of the ground.

Mitch continued: 'These were probably quite funny when they were installed – and I'm going by your definition of "funny', Bill, because shiny, bronze-coloured tree roots would look odd. But these are so dirty now they're indistinguishable from real roots so lots of people wouldn't even notice them. They might even trip over them and not realize they're supposed to be art.'

'Lots of people do get tripped up by art,' Bill quipped and looked pointedly at Mitch, who noticed the look and said:

'I'm serious – art has lost the plot.'

A hundred yards further along Mitch became animated and his voice boomed through the trees. They'd come across 'Seventy-one Steps' by David Nash: an artwork that did exactly what it said on the tin.

'This one gets me every time! Remind me, Bill, what is the one definition of art we can all agree upon?'

Bill sighed and resigned himself to the little exchange they always had when descending these wooden steps: 'Art should be useless.'

'Exactly! So how can this be art? They're steps aiding a descent down a hill.' He suddenly froze and his expression went into 'screensaver' mode, then he burst into animation again by patting his pockets and muttering, 'I've had an idea. I need to make a note of it and I've forgotten my notebook.'

'Use your phone.'

'I left my phone in the car.'

'Use mine.' Bill produced his smartphone from his jeans pocket.

Mitch hissed and made the sign of the cross with his two index fingers. 'Keep your devil works away from me. I only interact with dumb phones. Serves me right for not remembering my notebook. What sort of writer forgets to carry a notebook at all times? I'm going to trust my memory, I'm not senile yet,' and he gave up looking for any writing materials.

'What's the idea?'

'Good thinking, Bill, it will help me remember the idea later by talking about it now.

'It's occurred to me that contemporary art came into being as a revolt against representation. Human forms and shapes from nature were out and abstract concepts and shapes were in. It was fun for a while – making jokes and puzzles – but now contemporary art has run out of ideas. It's cycling round to return to representation. What has happened is that the natural environment is becoming *rare*. People in cities have forgotten what trees looks like and how wonderful they are so artists are now trying to remind them of it. As more of the natural environment is built upon and lost, the art we will go to admire will be real flowers and trees that will be "exhibited" in places like this park. I mean, look at that Penone piece over there...' They stared at a distant sculpture that looked just like a dead tree with a boulder stuck in its branches. 'That's a very good reproduction of a tree. It begs the question, why not just have a living tree there instead that's even more realistic than the artwork?'

As they crossed over the bridge above the weir at the end of the lake, Mitch was vocally exploring the ramifications of his thoughts in a stream of consciousness – he was enjoying himself. On the climb back up the open grassy hill to the main building they came across another new piece of sculpture.

'Oh dear,' said Mitch. 'Oh dear, oh dear.'

They were looking at a large sculpture of rusty metal framework about the size and shape of an HGV.

The interlocking, square-sectioned steel beams resembled the skeleton of a high-rise building before any floors or walls are attached, except in the sculpture none of the beams made any engineering sense. It was more like a giant puzzle.

Bill considered the piece. Finally he said, 'Well, it must be art because it's definitely useless.'

All that Mitch could do was mutter 'Oh dear, oh dear' over and over again.

As they walked back to the gift shop Mitch told Bill about a strange incident he'd witnessed the previous summer in the park.

'I was walking by the lake at the other end and there was a young chap protesting. Here's the funny thing, though. He was dressed all in black with a polo-neck jumper, black beret and dark glasses. He looked like a typical French avant-garde artist from the Sixties. He had a placard that said "THIS IS NOT ART" and he had a scarlet rope pegged up to run completely around himself so the public knew they weren't allowed to interact with him – except he interacted with them by shouting philosophical questions at them. I've never seen so many park wardens in one place with all their walkie-talkies crackling at the same time. Judging by their unease, I guessed it was some kind of unofficial stunt – probably by a performance art student. It was a good joke, though, and it got me thinking: I'm not the only one who thinks contemporary art has become a parody of itself.

'No, I'm going to feed off the decaying carcass of modern art by writing a story about it. When we get to the shop I'm going to find a scrap of paper or promotional leaflet and scribble this idea down using a pencil that's for sale in the gift shop – they can be hoist by their own petard!'

Eventually they reached the main building and on a counter Mitch found a white leaflet printed on matt cartridge paper with lots of blank sections. Inside the gift shop he found some pencils for sale and borrowed one to write his idea down for the story. As he scribbled, his thoughts seemed to tumble in on themselves and, as if in a hall of mirrors, they reflected back into infinity. He thought about the graphite in the pencil: he knew from history that at one time it was only available from two places in the world, one of which was in England. Then he thought about the wood encasing the pencil – wood that came from a living tree that has been sculpted into a hollow case to hold the graphite. He marvelled at the thought that some people might buy the pencil and then sketch trees with it on paper that was produced from dead trees. How ironic and perfect would that be? How useless an activity?

The Entertainers

I arrive over an hour early for my performance at the army camp. It's six o'clock on a December day and it's cold and dark as I walk from my car to the security hut. I feel a few spots of rain on my face. Once I'm through security I park up my car and make my way to the officers' mess. An orderly meets me and speaks to me using so many army slang words and acronyms that I barely understand a word he's saying. What I do understand of his monologue is along the lines of: 'Follow me and I'll show you the room where you need to wait until it's time for you to perform, but I'm just a dogsbody today and they treat me like shit so I don't suppose I'll get a drawing.'

I follow him along a lino-floored corridor then up a flight of black steps that have such a prominent strip of gripper on the leading edge of each step that they become a tripping hazard in themselves, and into a large, dimly lit recreational room. I look around the room and amid the easy chairs and coffee tables are TVs, pinball machines, table football and a pool table. I visualize the laughter and banter this place must generate when the men are on a break and relaxing with their mates, but now it is eerily silent. I notice the sudden rattle of heavy rain against the black, curtainless windows that run all around the room. I then catch sight of someone in an easy chair in the far corner – a young, dark-haired man looking at his phone.

The orderly says to me, 'That's John, he's juggling tonight. Someone will come and collect you both when it's time for you to perform.' And with that he leaves me.

I walk over to where John is sitting. From my forty years of working in the entertainment industry I don't recognize him and I'm sure I've never worked with him before. He senses my presence as I approach and he looks up from his phone, takes his earphones out and nods to me. He is clean-shaven, with a pudding face that just manages to keep out of the classification of 'unattractive' by virtue of his youth. I extend my arm and we shake hands while he remains seated. His handshake is unnervingly clammy to the touch and I have an urge to go and wash my hands immediately.

'I'm Ivor,' I say.

'John,' he comes back. He obviously didn't hear any of my conversation with the orderly at the door.

'I believe you're juggling this evening.'

'That's right. And what are you doing?'

I detect a mongrel accent.

'I'm caricaturing. Can you say "about" for me?'

'About.'

'Ah, you're American, not Canadian.'

'Oh my, that's well spotted. I haven't lived in the States for a long time.'

'How long have you been in the UK?'

'Eighteen years now.'

I place my coat and briefcase on the cushion of an easy chair next to him and I sit down in another easy chair beside my belongings. I feel we're in a waiting room to see some kind of doctor. John returns to his phone but I'm curious about him.

'Whereabouts in the States are you from?'

'From the East coast. Pittsburgh, Pennsylvania,' he says, still looking at his phone.

'And where have you travelled from tonight?'

'Bristol.'

'Do you miss living in the States?'

'Hell, no.' He says this with some force.

'Oh. Sorry, I didn't mean to pry.' I suddenly remember people can have lots of complicated reasons for leaving a place, not all of them benign.

John looks up from his phone, on which he appears to be playing some kind of game, and says, 'It's okay; I didn't mean it to sound so dramatic. Nothing unpleasant happened. I'm just a grumpy person.'

I am surprised by this frank admission and decide to follow the trail: 'Grumpy as in, just today or generally grumpy?' I ask, jokingly.

'Generally.'

'Hmm, that's fascinating. Coming from America, I'd expect you to be mega-enthusiastic about everything and over the top with your reactions. And you're an entertainer, too, so to claim you're grumpy... I mean, I don't want to fall into the trap of stereotyping you or anything, but that does surprise me.'

He merely shrugs. Then I think of something.

'Although, we need to qualify what we mean by grumpy. Being grumpy is a subjective viewpoint. Do you say you're grumpy because you feel that way or have other people pointed it out to you that you seem grumpy?'

'I've figured it out for myself. When I'm with a group of friends and they all seem to be having a great time I'm the guy who's thinking, what's all the fuss about? This is not so great.'

'Ah yes, I know what you mean. I'm similar. I always seem to have a negative attitude about a plan because I can see what's wrong with it. I'll say, "Yes, but what about this? It won't work because of this and this," and invariably, if they ignore my advice, I'll get proven right. Or if I'm watching what's supposed to be a highly rated film I'll be thinking, that's impossible, or absurd. Have you seen *The Revenant*, by the way?'

He shakes his head but I continue anyway: 'Some of the scenes in there are just risible. They're so absurd it spoiled the film for me.

'No, I have great difficulty in sharing popular views of what's good or supposed to be fun. Do you have difficulty identifying what fun is? I mean, are you having "fun" on your phone right now?'

He stops playing and looks at me before saying, 'No, I'm not having fun. Playing this game is a distraction from boredom. I play the game to kill time and killing time can't be seen as having fun.'

'I sometimes feel like that when I'm with a group of people – we're all killing time for our entire lives until the actual time comes for us to die. We just pretend the games we play are fun. I don't really understand what it means to feel as if you belong anywhere. It probably stems from my childhood: both my parents were immigrants and I've had a bicultural upbringing and now I don't identify with either culture. All my life I've felt on the outside of things, like a kid with his nose pressed against the window of a sweet shop.'

For the first time, John looks at me with his full attention and he says, 'There was a time in my life when I did feel I belonged to a group but that was during a period of heavy drug use so maybe it had more to do with the drugs than the people I was with. I'm quite a shy person, really.'

'Yes, so am I. I'm only confident now because I've learnt the skill of being confident. It's like juggling or drawing: if you keep practising you'll get better. Confidence is the same. You can fool people into believing you're super-confident when deep down, you're still shy. So why did you become an entertainer?'

'Well, it beats working for a living, for one thing. And I just kinda fell into it. One day I was doing magic tricks to impress people at parties and before I knew it I was juggling in Kuwait.'

'You know, I sometimes think that the people who become entertainers must have a common trait; the more entertainers I work with, the more I believe this. During our childhoods we must struggle to know what fun is so we seek out those experiences that are supposed to contain the most fun – things like performing in front of an audience – as a way of accessing it. We're like the drug addict moving onto harder drugs to achieve a bigger high. Entertainers are shy people who don't know what fun is so they look for it in the hardest drug in the world – public performance. I don't know about your experience but nearly all the entertainers I've met in my long career have had something odd about them. No disrespect.'

John dwells on this point before saying, 'Now that you mention it, yeah – I think you're right. Most of the people I know in the entertainment industry have an aura of dissatisfaction about them, like a distress signal. I'm going to change now.'

John stands up, goes behind a central wall where I can't see him and changes into a Robin Hood costume complete with bells. He reappears then practises some of his moves with his white juggling clubs. He has three of them. The low ceiling, however, is putting him off and he drops one. He tries to pick it up with a flick of his foot but the exaggerated curled point at the tip of the boot he's wearing interferes with the manoeuvre and the club misses his hand.

'It's not my costume,' he says, 'it was loaned to me by the agency, so I'm struggling to adapt some of my routine to it. I use my feet a lot in my routines.'

'Did you say you worked abroad? What was that like?' I ask.

'Yeah, Kuwait. I was young and naive at the time and it was my first experience abroad so I undercharged them. They treated me like shit, too – I think they just like ordering white folks around. I was there for three months and kept like a virtual prisoner. I came back with a lot of stress. I'm pretty sure it classified as PTSD.'

The orderly then appears in the doorway and tells us, 'You're wanted.'

Downstairs in the function room I'm sat in a corner next to the stage. A medieval banqueting table is set up in the centre of the room and couples take it in turns to leave the table and sit for me. They're all dressed in Robin Hood themed costumes ranging from filthy peasants to crowned kings.

Out of the corner of my eye I see John juggling by the side of the long table. He drops a club.

The man I'm drawing has a face full of distinctive features and I see the drawing come to life immediately. I can tell I'm on form tonight.

When I finish drawing the couple, I turn my clipboard round to show them the picture. I watch the look of astonishment suddenly develop on the man's face: 'That's fucking unbelievable!' he says. 'Bloody fantastic.'

The woman giggles hysterically.

I have a half smile on my face as I watch them marvel at the drawing, and I ask myself, am I having fun now? And I tell myself, no, this is not fun, I'm just doing my job entertaining people, and although I'm doing a very good job it's not what people would call fun. It's probably the nearest I'll ever get to it, though.

Afterwards, as I'm travelling home in a beautiful automobile to a beautiful wife, in a beautiful house (at least that's what the song playing on the radio is telling me) I think about my conversation with John. It was one of the most interesting I'd had with a fellow act: it gave me a small insight into who I might be.

As I approach diversion signs, I'm forced to switch off the cruise control and slow down to a crawl to join the queue of traffic being directed off the motorway.

I'm driving home alone in my two-year-old Ford Mondeo and I'm criss-crossing the motorway network of the country like thousands of other entertainers on a Saturday night in December. If I'm lucky, I'll get to meet a few of them during a gig that we're working on together, and I'll have snatched conversations with them.

We're always on the move, always searching for that next gig, for that validation that reassures us, *your life isn't wasted, you've been of service to others, and you've entertained them.*

I reflect on this as my Satnav recalculates the change in the planned route and tells me I've now got two hours and twenty minutes before I reach my destination. I'm already tired so the thought of so much driving makes me unhappy.

I'll probably never meet John again.

Death Date

After eighty-six years, two months and thirteen days, I can see the nascent light creep through my eyelids once more. I'm still here. This is going to be an interesting day.

The dawn penetrates my curtains with a growing boldness. I am experiencing the light of a new day for the 31,462nd time.

Will this be the last day I experience this amazing occurrence? As a young man I prophesied it would be and now the time has come. Today I die.

I was eighteen, hugely enjoying a foundation year in art college; I'd made some interesting new friends and discovered some talents I didn't even know I possessed. I was on the cusp of a wonderful future. Why, then, did I have the dream? It didn't make any sense.

I had never experienced another dream like it (nor have I experienced one since). The dream made me question which reality I inhabited: the sleep state or the waking? In the dream I was made aware of the date I would die: 19th October, 2018. The date carried such certainty that I never questioned it, not in my dream nor after I had woken up.

I told my family and friends about my dream but they just smiled or gave a little nod. It was as if, originating from a dream, the notion held little interest for them. (Any proof of the prophecy was still a lifetime away.) I could tell they thought I must have been drunk or have taken some psychoactive drug that produced the dream. It was their negative reaction that made me get the tattoo.

I felt I needed to demonstrate the validity of the revelation given to me, so I went to a tattoo parlour and had the date inked into my skin just below my right ankle. It appears on a drawing of a gravestone with my name on it: Steven Manthorp, 19.10.2018. RIP.

I had it inked on that part of my anatomy to assist the attendant in the mortuary: as part of their routine they normally tie a cardboard label to the big toe of the cadaver with the date of death on it. I figured they would see the tattoo and realize I'd saved them a job. If they were superstitious they might even think I had precognition and would therefore need to be wary around my cadaver in case I possessed powers that escaped the confines of death.

From that day onwards my conversations with people I'd just met took one of two turns: if I sensed they were 'straight' I kept to the small talk and never mentioned my death date. If, however, I decided the person was 'interesting' I might bring up subjects that were off the beaten track and one of those subjects would inevitably be my dream of the death date (I realize now I was subconsciously looking for others who might have had a similar experience). If the person found the idea fascinating but ultimately inconsequential, I'd show them my heel with the tattoo. Having the date committed to permanent ink made them reappraise my conviction.

And now 19.10.2018 has arrived.

As I lie in bed I mentally go over my health issues to see if any could precipitate my sudden death: my heart bypass operation from years ago, my chronic hip pain, my digestive troubles, that scratch I received from a thorn bush last week that might develop into sepsis – none of them seem to be serious enough to make me think I could drop dead today. I still feel as if I have enough energy to make it through another twenty-four hours, easy. But of course, people suddenly drop dead all the time: from aneurisms, heart attacks, allergic reactions... they never see it coming.

So if not a health issue, could it be an accident that catches me unawares? I have no plans to drive anywhere today, although a trip to the shops later is not out of the question; and all it takes is one careless young motorist busy looking at their phone and—poof! Life is erased. But I'm not so steady on my feet, now; clumsiness is something I have to watch out for. A second handrail was attached to the stairs in my home years ago. All it would take is a little stumble at the top of the stairs and a headfirst tumble down them and... Oh, I suppose I could go on and on imagining possible scenarios, and what good would it do me? For all I know, it might be my wife, Cindy, who decides to run a knife through me in a fit of rage. She might have recently learned of my infidelity and go berserk. Actually, she's more likely to murder me for an unguarded comment I might make about her slovenliness – her irascibility often tips her over the edge these days.

I have to confess, during the last few months, as the day approached, I could think of little else than of what might happen today – how will I die? The dream told me nothing of that part. At first, I consoled myself with congratulations on making it so far – eighty-six is a good innings and at least I hadn't died years before the date inked on my foot. That would have been an embarrassing tragedy – I mean, my prophecy would have been proven wrong *and* I'd have lived less than I imagined I was due.

A part of me feels I should be elated at the prospect of cheating my own death date (and the subsequent days of life a bonus) but another part of me will feel betrayed if the date is false; the dream *promised* this date.

Then a weird thing happens – I begin to question the reality I'm experiencing and I ask myself, how can I be sure I haven't died in my sleep already and this is an afterlife? I mean, if in the dream I was certain of the death date, it stands to reason that this apparent wakefulness could also be an utterly convincing illusion. Maybe when I meet Cindy in the kitchen in a short while and we have breakfast I'll know for sure. All it will take is one look of scorn from her and I'll know I'm still alive in the 'real' world.

A large part of my brain says, 'get up!' but another part tells me to 'stay in bed, your life is over, you've nothing to get up for'. And I am tired of life. The news on TV always looks like old news to me, repeated every thirty years or so. All the novelty has gone from my existence. When was the last time I laughed? Really laughed. I don't know. Even the absurdity of existence has lost its appeal. Perhaps that's how I'll die today; my body will just give up the ghost, all my cells will realize there's no point carrying on and the machine will just shut down.

Or, on the other hand, I could be proactive and make this a day to remember – a damn good day to die.

I look at my tablets on the bedside cabinet. I get up from my bed. This is going to be an interesting day.

Ten Thousand Light Years from Home

Ahmad felt the urge to pee. He thought about peeing in his pants. He was so comfortable sat in one of the most comfortable chairs ever invented that he felt disinclined to move. But then he thought the pee would start to turn cold after a bit and he wouldn't want that – it would ruin everything.

It was very early in the morning, he wasn't sure what time exactly, but he could just make out the faint suggestion of a sunrise over the black expanse of ocean. Through the windshield there was only one point of light visible to him anywhere – the moon was up in the sky to his left and he stared at it.

Men have stood on that piece of dry rock, he thought, but only a handful.

How he wished he could be on the moon right now, on his own, a quarter of a million miles away from Earth, staring at the blue-and-white marble hanging in space. He shivered even though the air in the cabin was 24 degrees Celsius.

He got out of the pilot's chair and moved towards the cockpit door. The plane was on autopilot, as it had been for the past five hours, so he didn't need to worry about leaving the controls unattended. He had to push hard against the door to overcome an obstruction on the other side.

As he made his way down the aisle of passengers to the toilet, the cabin was silent underneath the ever-present white noise of the jet engines.

There was a nearer toilet in the first-class section of the plane but he liked to walk down the length of the aisle because it made him feel like he owned the territory – as if he were a country squire walking the boundary of his estate. He'd worked hard all his life to get where he was and as a respected captain with thirty years' service he felt he deserved it. I mean, what is the point of working so hard if you can't indulge yourself now and again, he thought.

He passed one woman, sitting next to a small girl – presumably her young daughter - who reminded him of his wife. The woman's lush dark hair tumbled loosely over her shoulders. She was very attractive – just like his wife had once been.

Of course, the bitch wasn't good looking anymore, despite all the money she'd spent – *his money*, on spas, cosmetic surgery and beauty treatments. After all the things he'd given her she just ups and leaves him to rattle around inside the big house he'd bought for them to grow old in together. She must have poisoned his daughters' ears too when she left as they had visited him precisely once in the last two years. Oh, sure, they were adults and had their own careers now but surely they could find a day or two to visit their father. Even in the early years of his career, with his insanely busy schedule, he had managed to spend some time at home.

He entered the toilet and relieved himself. After he'd finished he didn't bother flushing it.

As he walked back along the aisle to the cockpit he stopped for a moment to admire the novel view of the oxygen masks dangling from the overhead compartments. They had dropped down hours ago when he'd temporarily depressurized the cabin. His imagination had started to form an analogy about the oxygen lines being the strings of a grand puppeteer operating the mindless puppets below, when he suddenly felt a shudder from the aircraft. The jet engines coughed and whined and he realized it was nearly time.

As he approached the cockpit door he looked down and noticed the obstruction that had given him such trouble when he'd headed for the toilet – his young co-pilot, slumped on the floor. He looked smart in his white shirt and blue tie.

Back in the cockpit, he sat back in his seat again and prepared himself. An incessant alarm was sounding. He'd have liked to shut it off but he knew it was impossible to override the *low fuel* messages. He'd just have to put up with it.

He took the plane out of autopilot and under manual control. He eased the nose of the aircraft downwards and his windshield view filled with nothing but vast empty ocean. The sky had lightened considerably in the few minutes he'd spent visiting the toilet and he could clearly see the black water stretching in every direction around him. His flight plan was coming to its conclusion.

In his own way, he told himself, he was an adventurer travelling to a place very few people had ever visited. He'd had the idea of going to this place for a while now. It fascinated him. It was unthinkable. It was the only thing that interested him and the only place left for him to visit.

So, this is it, he thought. *I'm arriving at last. Is it going to be as exquisite a place as I imagine? I'm in the middle of the southern ocean with a plane full of dead people – I'm so far beyond the realms of human imagination that even the compassion of Allah can't reach me. Nothing can.*

Then the plane hit the water.

The Delivery

'Hi Jake, it's Lucien. I wonder if you could do me a favour.'

'I'll try. What is it?'

I was standing in my front room looking out of the window into the cul-de-sac of the street where I live. Across the circle of orange paving bricks that constitute the road I could see Jake standing in the front room of his detached house holding a cordless telephone that, seconds before, he'd just picked up from a cradle sitting on his windowsill. On learning it was me calling, he turned to look in the direction of my house and saw me standing at my window. Ordinarily I'd have walked the forty metres to his house to speak with him, but only if I saw him out and about in the garden or drive, which he often is as he's retired. If I don't see him out in his garden I think it's more polite to telephone him rather than go knocking on his door as it's easier for him to ignore the telephone than someone at the door should he choose to be undisturbed.

'Are you going to be in on Thursday this week, around lunchtime?'

'As far as I'm aware.'

'Ah, right. I've got a delivery coming that day and they can't give me a more specific time than between nine a.m. and five p.m. I'm in for most of the day but I need to pop out at lunchtime. If they turn up at that time they won't be able to deliver. I wonder if you could keep an eye out for the delivery van, for about an hour.'

'Thursday... Let me think. I'm at the dentist in the morning but I'll be back about eleven. Yes, that's fine, no problem.'

'I'll leave a note on my door but I'll have to leave you my garage key so you can unlock the door and put the item in there.'

'Why don't you just tell them to deliver the parcel to number five?'

'It's a large item, which is why it needs to go into my garage.'

Jake looked over at me with his phone held up to his ear. It was as if he was waiting for me to go on. As I didn't, he then said, 'I see. What is it, a fridge or something?'

'No, it's, um...' I suddenly realized I hadn't prepared a suitably vague response to such a specific question and I thought about saying it was a piece of furniture (which it kind of was) to deflect the question. But then I considered the possibility of him taking receipt of the delivery and recognizing the unmistakable shape of the item and his surprise that I hadn't mentioned what it was earlier, so I said, 'It's, er, a coffin.'

From forty metres away I saw Jake's head – which in that instant had been idly looking in the direction of his front garden as if assessing the work he would need to do in the springtime – immediately jerk in my direction so he had direct eye contact with me.

'Did I hear you correctly? Did you just say "a coffin"?'

'Yes, I did.'

Jake then gave a short nervous laugh and said, 'Is there something more I need to know about your business activities or should I not breathe a word to anyone about this?' Then he had a thought. 'Is it a coffin for a pet dog? Although, having said that, you don't have a dog, do you...?'

His comment made me suddenly curious and I said, 'Hm, do they make coffins for dogs? Anyway, never mind. No, it's not for an animal, it's for a person.'

'Oh dear. Do I... I mean, should I... Is everything all right?'

'Yes, yes, don't worry, Jake, no one in my immediate family's died. It's my mother-in-law who's died.'

'Your mother-in-law has died? I'm sorry to hear that but why are *you* having a coffin delivered to your house? Don't the undertakers take care of all that business?'

'In this instance, no undertaker is involved.'

'No undertaker? So how is the funeral going to take place?'

'There isn't going to be a funeral.'

I could see Jake studying me and weighing up his next words carefully as he tried to interpret my expression from such a distance. I fully expected him to keep to form and repeat what I'd just said.

'Forgive me – and tell me if it's none of my business – but I'm puzzled as to how it's possible to have someone die and for there not to be a funeral.'

'The two things are mutually exclusive. It's one of those common misconceptions about death but, contrary to popular belief, you're not obliged to hire an undertaker or book a funeral if you don't want to. It's like probate or buying a house – you can do these things yourself but most people never consider the option because they never think to ask if they can.'

'No funeral...?' I could sense Jake struggling with the idea, like a fish being told there's such a thing as water. He continued: 'Was that what your mother-in-law wished for in her will – no funeral?'

I gave a heavy sigh and decided to be straight with him. 'She didn't leave any instructions, nothing. Not even a will. And anyway, Jake, there'd be no point in having a funeral because no one would be there, not even her children.'

Jake was now studying me through the window as if I had just transformed into a lizard before his very eyes.

There was a long silence before he said, 'can I ask why?'

'My mother-in-law was a very troubled person, Jake. She had no friends, not one. And... even her three children despised her.'

'But you told me she was a published author with TV deals and such like. Surely she'd have *someone* who would miss her and want to pay their respects.'

'Yes, you'd think so, but authors are weird people – at least, most of the ones my wife met through her mother when she still lived with her. They spend long hours locked up in a room constructing fantasy worlds that they control with absolute power. I'm not sure if it's the writing that makes authors the way they are or if it's the already weird people who are attracted to writing because of the control it gives them. I suppose someone from her publishing company might have turned up to her funeral when she was being productive but it's been so long since she wrote anything new that they wouldn't consider it a priority. I tell you what though... I secretly think she would have relished this whole improbable scenario – almost as if it were lifted from one of her own bizarre detective novels.'

'I'm flabbergasted. I didn't even imagine such things went on in the world. So what's going to happen? To her, I mean – how is she going to be... disposed of?'

'One of her sons has organized everything. He still lives in the area. He's ordered the coffin over the internet

– they're a lot cheaper online. It's coming here because he hasn't the room to store it anywhere at his house and I said we would help out. He's booked a slot at the crematorium so he's getting everything ready. On the day before the cremation he's going to hire a Transit van that he'll then use to pick up the coffin from here. The following morning, he'll drive to the morgue, put his mother into the coffin, then drive to the crematorium and have it burnt.'

Jake looked appalled. 'He's going to handle the body of his mother…?'

I felt I had to quickly change the subject to something less distasteful so I added, 'Did you know there's such a thing as ash cash?'

'No, what is it?' he said mechanically, still thinking about the body being placed inside the coffin.

'Well, before the body can be cremated, two doctors have to sign it off as safe to burn. The crematoriums don't want pacemakers or whatever exploding in the furnace. The form takes a few minutes to fill in and I'm not sure why it takes two doctors to do the honours but they charge nearly a hundred and fifty pounds for the form. It's required by law, so it's essentially a licence for them to print money. I've read that the doctors have a piss-up every Friday when they receive the money from that week's form-filling. It's amazing what you discover when you research things – things that people take for granted. I suspect when people hire an undertaker they won't even question the undertaker's itemized bill when it's delivered to the relatives.'

Even from a distance of forty metres it was possible to see the expression on Jake's face; he was like a fish that had been told that not only was there such a thing as water but that other fish defecate in it. I realized I might have said too much so I tried to bring the conversation to a speedy close and gain his cooperation. 'So, would you be okay keeping an eye out for the delivery?'

A weary, resigned sigh hissed through my earpiece before Jake said, 'Yeah, fine. Happy to help.'

On Thursday, the coffin arrived at lunchtime when I was out. Jake had opened my garage door with the key I'd left him and the van driver had placed it in there.

I retrieved the key from Jake and opened my garage to inspect the coffin. It was made from cardboard so I was worried about possible transit damage. After a quick inspection that everything was okay, I read the white label stuck on the plastic wrapping:

Cardboard Coffin. Small. Rope handles.
Brown, Economy.

I imagined my mother-in-law soon inhabiting the coffin. Then I thought about her son who was to place her in it and what his feelings might be towards her. I imagined he had a mental label that he would attach to her as he finished his task:

Dead person. Small. No friends.
Wrote stories.

If you enjoyed *Sex and Death & Other Stories,* why not try our other Armley Press titles? Available in Kindle and paperback from Amazon, and through UK bookshops.

Ray Brown: *In All Beginnings*

P. James Callaghan: *Thurso*

Mark Connors: *Stickleback*

Mark Connors: *Tom Tit and the Maniacs*

A.J. Kirby: *The Lost Boys of Prometheus City*

John Lake: *Hot Knife*

John Lake: *Blowback*

John Lake: *Speedbomb*

John Lake: *Amy and the Fox*

Mick McCann: *Coming Out as a Bowie Fan in Leeds, Yorkshire, England*

Mick McCann: *Nailed*

Mick McCann: *How Leeds Changed the World: Encyclopaedia Leeds*

Chris Nickson: *Leeds, the Biography: A History of Leeds in Short Stories*

Nathan O'Hagan: *The World is (Not) a Cold Dead Place*

Nathan O'Hagan: *Out of the City*

Samantha Priestley: *Reliability of Rope*

Samantha Priestley: *A Bad Winter*

David Siddall: *Breaking Even*

K.D. Thomas: *Fogbow and Glory*

Michael Yates: *20 Stories High*

Visit us at armleypress.com and look for Armley Press on Facebook and Twitter.

Lightning Source UK Ltd.
Milton Keynes UK
UKHW011840291019
352558UK00001B/45/P